EVER GREEN

AL ROJO

Copyright © A L Rojo 2026

The moral right of the author has been asserted in accordance with the Copyright Amendment (Moral Rights) Act 2000.

All rights reserved. Except as permitted under the Australian Copyright Act 1968 (for example, fair dealing for the purposes of study, research, criticism or review) no part of this publication may be reproduced, stored in a retrieval system, or transmitted in any form or by any means, electronic, mechanical, photocopying, recording or otherwise, without the written permission of the publisher.

https://www.nla.gov.au/collections

Title: Ever Green

Author: Rojo, A L

ISBNs:

978-0-6488690-7-8 (paperback)

Subjects:

FICTION: Romance/Paranormal/Shifters; Fantasy/Romance; Romance/Fantasy; Fantasy/General

This story is entirely a work of fiction. No character in this story is taken from real life. Any resemblance to any person or persons living or dead is accidental and unintentional. The author, their agents and publishers cannot be held responsible for any claim otherwise and take no responsibility for any such coincidence.

Cover concept by A L Rojo

Cover design by Dovnik Designs

Formatting by Page Turner Studios

ALSO BY A L ROJO

The Pack of Farrowline Series

The Heart of Farrowline

The Power of Farrowline

The Strength of Farrowline

The Pride of Farrowline

The Duty of Farrowline

Shifters of Azanir Series

The Lost Lady of the Darkwoods

The Found Lady of Azanir

Standalone Novels

Ever Green

AUTHOR NOTE

Ever Green contains themes/chapters of abuse, assault, violence, explicit language and adult content. This novel is intended for adult readers.

Please head to www.alrojo.com.au for all content warnings and information on all of my novels.

DEDICATION

To those who never dreamt of being the princess but the hero who went on the quest

CHAPTER ONE

'Move!'

'I am!'

Ducking and rolling, I hop backwards just in time to miss the sword that cuts the air close to my chest. I feel the rush of adrenaline and roll along the dirt and come up into a perfect crouch.

Panting, I glare at the elderly warrior shaking his thick head at me like I'm the one who's doing the wrong thing. 'You could've gutted me!' I shout, genuinely enraged and shocked when I look down at my tunic to see a thin slice along the material.

'If I wanted to gut you, girl, you wouldn't be breathing.'

Muttering curses under my breath, I inspect the damage to my shirt. 'You know Anna is going to be angry at me now.'

My maid is a grumpy, always busy and always gossiping, pain in my butt. The one thing that sets her off the most is when I come back with my clothes ruined from training. I can just hear her reprimand at how a 'lady shouldn't fight.'

She says it every day as if she is unaware of the situation I am in and how important it is for me to at least learn some form of self-defence. It's not like I actually put myself in training to begin with anyway. My father set this all up for me years ago, after I was kidnapped as a child and my mother was killed. You can't say no when he tells you to do something. Not that I'd ever test that theory. My loyalty is to my King.

My father.

For him, and for this kingdom, I will learn how to wield a sword, even when I'm not that good with one. I'll wear ugly dresses and smile when I'm in a room of court nobles who whisper behind their hands and throw comments under their breath that they know I can hear perfectly well.

Even now, when all seems helpless, I'll keep being the daughter he demands that I be.

'You're distracted today, Susyri. I know you're concerned about the King, but you must be on high alert. Times are only going to get darker if he succumbs to this illness. You will need every advantage you have. Your history should have you taking this seriously.' He isn't wrong. My life is spiralling and I have no way of controlling the speed of my downfall.

'I'm trying, Master Kieran.' I sound as sad as I feel and I sit heavily on the dirt of the training ring we are using at the back of the royal estate. There are soldiers everywhere, going about their business or sparring. It's busy today. No one pays any attention to me. I'm down here a lot and looking in my direction normally gets people in trouble.

Kieran Hawkins offers me a sympathetic look that just makes matters worse. The big, bulky soldier has been in my life since the moment I moved onto the castle grounds. He was once the commander of the army and recently retired to make way for the 'younger generation'.

You wouldn't think the word 'old' or a man ready for retirement when you look at him. He's built like a tree, doesn't take shit from anyone and knows how to kill with his bare hands. He's one of my father's trusted men and has taught me everything I know about combat and defence.

His job lately is to ensure my safety. Having Kieran around has felt like having a real father.

Last month, when I was caught drinking too much at the summer festival and found myself in the arms of a random solider, it was Kieran who reprimanded me while holding back my hair as I threw up. It was disgusting and a little funny. I haven't touched the stuff since, which I know he and Anna are very happy about.

'I don't know what I'm going to do, Kieran. I really don't.' The lump in my throat makes it hard to say any more.

My father is sick. Really sick. I'd give and do anything to help him recover.

Anything.

CHAPTER TWO

Cradling my father's head, I bring the small goblet of water to his lips and help him to drink.

Lowering him gently back against the pillow, I hold his too warm hand, my voice a whisper as I tell him everything I promise to do if he just gets better.

I vow I'll train harder. I'll stop getting into arguments. I reluctantly agree, if he wakes, to discuss the betrothal I've been arguing with him about for the last six months.

'Please, just wake up. You know I cannot survive without you. This kingdom needs you.'

I still can't believe that this is happening.

Five days ago, he was walking around the halls with his swords strapped to his hip and his voice booming off the stone walls of the castle.

In five days, he went from a man in his prime to this.

I search the paleness of his complexion for some kind of clue as to what has happened.

The dark circles under his eyes were not there yesterday and his face seems to be sinking into his bones. I insisted that a healer be called when I first walked into this room and demanded that they look over him for the hundredth time.

They can't tell me anything though.

Just like me, they're perplexed by what's happening to our King.

Head bowed, I plead softly to the heavens to help me. 'I'd do anything,' I whisper. 'Please give me the answers to heal my father.' Ignoring the small commotion behind me, I grip my father's hand harder and hope that someone listens to my prayer.

'What are you doing in here? Who let you in?' The voice that booms from the doorway ignites that ever boiling pot of anger in my chest. I don't have to look over my shoulder to know who is there and the dramatic entourage of soldiers she has brought with her. She has spies everywhere. It's just another game.

It's always a game.

I force myself to breathe and not react. Starting an argument would go against the promises I just made to the King. I said I'd do better, so I need to. Even if every fibre of my being wants to retaliate and snap at the bitch.

'I'm visiting my father,' I state instead, keeping my voice steady. It does no one any good if I showed her the true extent of my emotions.

I don't know how it's possible, but the already high pitched, annoying voice kicks up a notch. 'Don't you dare call him that! Get out!'

Sighing heavily, I pay no attention to the heavy footsteps that stop behind my chair.

The soldier now behind me is in the Queen's pocket and will do her bidding despite who I am and my father's commands that I am never to be touched.

A fragile command that will shatter the moment he stops breathing.

Kissing the hand still within mine, I send one more silent plea to the heavens for my father to recover. A selfish request as I know I won't survive this hell without him.

I stand, back straight, defiant.

Refusing to look at the heavily armed soldier or the ones in the doorway eying me off to see what I'll do, I steel my spine and march out of the King's chamber with a look towards the Queen that I hope cuts her as deep as I intend it to.

It's pointless though. A witch like her has the skin of an ogre.

I feel instantly bad the moment I think that— poor witches and ogres don't deserve to be compared to *her*.

Forcing myself to stay calm, I stride from the room without bowing, which I'm sure will bite me in the arse later, but who cares.

If my father dies, I have bigger things to worry about than getting chewed out because I didn't bow to *Her Majesty*.

CHAPTER THREE

Too lost in grief and despair, I pick the path back through the lavish gardens and fountains of the estate to the apartments that contain my rooms.

The moon is high and I decide not to rush. Dinner will be long over, so there's nothing to hurry for. Not that I've been eating much these last few days. The weight of my circumstance and the fear for my future sits like steel in my stomach.

Contemplating my very limited life choices, I jump when a musical voices speaks from the darkness. 'I know how to cure your father.'

Grabbing the hilt of my sword, I swing around, heart in my throat and stop dead at the sight before me.

There on the path I just walked is the most beautiful woman I've ever seen.

Wide eyed, I monitor each step she takes over the gravel path and note the absence of sound. My eyes frantically search the space above her shoulders to ensure she's not what my brain is screaming she could be.

Her long, white-blonde hair falls effortlessly to her hips, the colour so unnaturally perfect that I take an involuntary step back. The only thing keeping me from running for my life is that she appears to be human and not... *one of them*.

Her silver gown sways on a phantom breeze and I grip the hilt in my hand and try to calm my breathing. Her eyes match her gown and they are fixed on me. She smiles and the adrenaline that was pumping in my veins calms slightly as the light around her seems to dull until I begin to believe that I imagined her otherworldliness.

'Sorry Lady, what did you say?' I ask, reprimanding my overactive imagination because the woman that strides gracefully towards me is just another noble.

Looking around, my brow furrows at the fact that she's alone. You wouldn't find a noble lady out in the garden at night like this, not without an escort.

Me on the other hand, I'm a bastard. I'm not that important, or so the Queen finds necessary to keep reminding me.

'I apologise for startling you, Susyri. I said that I know how you can save your father.'

Opening my mouth to reply, I'm stopped by a manicured hand. She raises it so eloquently that I become transfixed by the fluidity of her movement.

'I am sorry but time is limited, and I have a great deal to say. And you must listen carefully. The only way to save your father is with the blood of the Alpha Lord and ruler of the Ekalus.'

An involuntary gasp escapes my lips just before I can catch it. I take another step away from her. My mind screams at me to run, but my feet feel as if they're stuck.

The *Ekalus*.

The shifter monsters that haunt our people.

They are evil. They're demons who are said to change their form to that of a mighty bird of prey. Some say the males can half-shift so they appear like a human in the body with demon wings.

They are predators.

'Susyri, you have to follow the Tilman Road until you reach the Dead Forest. You need to find the gift returned and get past the monster that guards the road out. Get to the top of Ekalus Peak. Only then will you be granted an audience with the Alpha Lord. When you are there, tell him your story. Tell him of your lineage and what has happened here tonight. Show him this,' she states, lifting an exquisitely crafted necklace. The heavy looking emerald stone set within the swirling vines of gold is stunning. The green is vibrant and rich, captivating.

I don't know at what part of the story my jaw hits the floor. I have to find the strength to lift it up before I can find the words to reply to the mysterious woman. Her eyes are hard and serious while they watch me.

'The Alpha Lord?' I question. She doesn't move or confirm, just stands, waiting. 'As in the Lord of the Ekalus? But those soulless winged demons don't care about us mortals. They sit on their mountains unconcerned by us. One hasn't been seen in generations. And you want me to go up to the *Alpha Lord*?

The leader of all those predators and say what? Hey Sir, do you reckon you could cut your palm and give me some of that healing blood of yours so that I can save my father, the human King, from a mysterious illness that is killing him slowly and painfully?' Laughing at the absurdity of what I'm hearing, I release the handle of my weapon, now very confident that this woman is not a threat—a lunatic maybe— but not dangerous.

I don't miss the flash of anger on her face or the way the necklace sways as it dangles from her outstretched hand.

'Good day, Lady. I'd suggest you find your rooms. It's late and I don't know where the soldiers who are stationed here are. It may not be safe. Especially carrying such an expensive jewel.'

Dipping my head in respect, I turn on my heel with the intent of leaving.

I'm stopped by a hand on my arm. The grip like a vice. The heat of the touch burns.

I gasp and spin around.

Snapping my gaze back to those silver eyes, my insides churn at the threat in her tone as she says, 'you must only travel to Ekalus Peak through the Tilman Road and then through the Dead Forest. Find the gift returned. Get past the monster guarding the road. No other way. And you must start this quest alone, Susyri. This is your journey to take.'

'Right.' This lady needs help. 'So, not only am I to travel to Ekalus Peak to visit the winged demons that'll kill me on sight just for fun, but you're also saying that the only way I can get to them is on the most notorious road in the kingdom.

The Tilman Road is mostly used by robbers and bandits and the villages along the road are said to be some of the most dangerous to visit. Then, you want me to go through a place called the *Dead* Forest. A forest I've never heard about and I've been educated by the best tutors in the castle. Along the way I have to find the gift returned, then defeat a monster. All on my own? Good night, Lady,' I finish through gritted teeth, my patience now well and truly at its end.

'You must start this journey *alone*, Susyri,' she emphasises like I need to understand that, more than any of the other details. 'This journey is yours.'

'You've said that.' I've had enough.

Storming away from the figure that stands unnaturally still, watching me, I hurry through the gardens and past the barracks to the apartments beside the busy area. The noisy hall, filled with castle workers and soldiers, is lively tonight and I hurry up the large stairs and to the sanctuary of my modest apartment. Thank the universe that I'm alone.

Slamming the door, I lock it quickly. Back against the wood, I find myself unable to shake the feeling that I just escaped a danger more frightening than the idea of going on a journey to a place called the Dead Forest to fight a monster. Then to Ekalus Peak.

The Ekalus. Half humans who can shift their form, sprout massive wings, and turn into birds of prey. It is said the male Ekalus are as deadly as the beasts they look like.

That is how the stories go.

Myth and reality are probably two different things when it comes to the tales of the Ekalus. Some stories say the shifters stay as humans when they sprout the demon wings, others say they completely change into monstrous-sized birds. Body and all.

I say, 'let's leave the demons alone and we'll all live happily ever after'. I shudder at the thought of going anywhere near Ekalus Peak. The mountains in the distance from the city, can stay in the distance. I've never seen one of the winged demons, actually it's been a few generations since one has been spotted, or so the tales sung in the city say. However, you get those travelling minstrels or gossipers in the barracks who tell stories of villages ravaged by a Ekalus monster. Women taken. Houses burnt. Men killed.

From what I've heard, there is no purpose to their destruction. The stories might differ about what they look like but there is one thing they all have in common, they're no friend to humans.

There is no way I will be going anywhere near one.

CHAPTER FOUR

'Your father is worse today, Susyri. I'm sorry,' Kieran states. I knew the moment he and Father Fredrick came around that something was wrong. It is too early for visitors.

Father Fredrick was a friend of my late mothers.

The King's mistress.

He promised to watch over me, or so he says. The tall, grey-haired man, all arms and legs, preaches peace and charity but carries a knife under his robes. He might look like a man you could push over with a light shove but I've seen him defend a member of his congregation like a mother bear with her cubs. I've known him my entire life.

Nodding while holding back the dam of tears that threaten to explode, I thank Anna when she places a cup and saucer of tea before me. My guests are fully aware of the battle raging within me. How could they not? They mumble their thanks when they're served. Anna just mutters a reply and heads to the small kitchen she hates using. I really don't know why I keep her on.

She was directed by my father to serve me, so I didn't question it. I'm not even sure I'm allowed to release her from my service.

'Have you decided what you will do?'

'No.' I sigh. 'He'll be all right. My father can't die. It's not his time.'

Laying his very large hand over the one I have on the table, Kieran offers me a small smile. 'The King will need a miracle to survive this. You have to start planning what you'll do when…if—' my adviser corrects when he sees me flinch, '—if he passes.'

'We believe that you should leave the moment it happens. If you'd let us arrange it, we'll move you to the country as far from this place as possible and out of the Queen's reach,' Father Fredrick exclaims. He's been very concerned about my wellbeing since my father fell ill.

'This kingdom is too unstable. There is no telling what will happen when the King dies.'

They nod their heads in agreement. I trust their advice. They've taught me how to survive in this ruthless court as the illegitimate and only child of the King. They're the only evidence that my father cares really.

I love the King and try to be the dutiful daughter but most days it's hard to tell if that love is reciprocated.

'He needs a miracle,' I ponder, taking a sip of tea. I hate the small voice that whispers, *'he needs the blood of the Alpha Lord,'* in my mind. The words of the strange woman from the other night consumes my thoughts and makes it hard to stay within the conversation happening around the small table.

'Susyri, you don't have very many options. I've contacted a lovely family in the country who are willing to take you in. They're members of my parish. I trust them to keep you safe and look after you until we can get you out of the kingdom.'

My heart stutters. 'Out of the kingdom?'

'Yes, Susyri.' Father Fredrick gives me that sympathetic look that always makes me uncomfortable. I hate sympathy. I know my life hangs in the balance. It has since the Queen found out I existed at the age of ten, when my mother was murdered and I was taken. I've heard stories of how my father sent hordes of soldiers to look for me and killed my captors himself. I don't have many memories of what happened. It changed my entire life though.

The Queen never had any children and I suffer every day like it's my fault.

'You can't possibly think that anywhere in the kingdom would be safe with your father dead.'

'Susyri,' Kieran states, drawing my attention away from Father Fedrick. The old man looks wary as if what he's about to say might make me upset. 'I want you to consider the betrothal to Lord Highben. His family has power and influence and he lives far over the ocean. They can protect you.'

Face scrunching up, I fight the need to act like a child. 'He's much older than I am,' I say, instead of confessing how I hated the way he looked at me when he visited last winter. It made me uncomfortable. He was handsome enough. Brown eyes, tall, knew how to hold a sword.

He dressed nicely and had broad shoulders, but he didn't...make me smile, or feel anything, really. Lord Hamish Highben is just another noble.

I know it'll never happen, but I want...more.

A stupid fantasy imagined by a girl who hasn't felt love and tenderness in a very long time.

CHAPTER FIVE

The reality of my situation weighs heavily on my soul while I prepare for sleep that night. Death will not come quickly if my father dies. The Queen has too much influence in court because of the lies she continually sprouts about me. I know my end will be painful and drawn out.

Father Fredrick informed me that it's whispered the Queen is already preparing for the day she'll become the leader of our kingdom. Most of the court believe that she's worthy to take the crown.

Yes, I have supporters. However, most of them are nobles I barely know. They probably think they can 'control' me in some way if they put me on the throne. The thing no one seems to understand is that I have no time or desire to play those games.

I genuinely don't want to be the Queen. I just want to be left alone. I have no desire to be anything but me, Susyri Oakwell, not Susyri Oakwell-Harchon, the King's bastard daughter. I'd give up this life in a heartbeat to become a commoner, free to do what I want.

Unable to calm my mind, I pace back and forth, running my hands along the many surfaces in my apartment. The moon creates shadows as it filters through the open space and I stop at the table Kieran and Father Fredrick were sitting around a few hours ago trying to come up with a plan.

Studying the map of the kingdom Kieran left behind, I run my finger along the Tilman Road. It starts just outside the city and runs nearly the full length of the kingdom.

I follow the map all the way until the end of the road. It forks out, a new road going one way and the other seems to be a dead end.

My finger finds Ekalus Peak next.

The home of the Ekalus.

Drawing my hand back, I clench my fist, unsure why my heart is now pounding. I have no desire to come face-to-face with an immortal, winged hunter who views mortals as lesser. Yet, I can't stop thinking about what that woman said to me. *Does it make me selfish to be too afraid to even contemplate facing the Alpha Lord who reigns over those predators?*

I am nobody.

Yes, I can fight and I'm trained. I know about this kingdom and have been educated like the daughter of a King should be, but I'm no warrior.

I don't even think that I'd make it to the end of the Tilman Road if I tried. And the Dead Forest is not a place on this map or any that I've seen in my life.

Annoyed at myself for even thinking that I should be listening to that lunatic, I push the map off the table and stomp to the window.

With everything that's happening, I'm worried that my life is spiralling out of control. The problem is that it's been stuck in this whirlwind since my mother died and I was dragged here to live on the estate.

I don't think I've ever truly recovered from the loss.

My mother was beautiful. There were moments in my life when I wished for her height and her gorgeous shiny, pale skin.

I got my father's tanned complexion, his grey eyes and his round face. I don't know where my short height came from. The only real gift I got from my mum is my hair. It flows down my back in a thick wavy mass. The midnight colour is all her and there are times when I can't bear to look at myself in the mirror.

Afraid for my future and knowing deep down that I have no options, I rest my head on the glass of the window and sigh. The thought for my own safety makes me feel selfish. My father is in the castle right now, on the other side of the garden, on his deathbed, and I'm here sad for my own life.

I hate myself for being so self-centred.

The glass shakes with a rumble of unexpected thunder and I jump back from the window with a gasp. The world outside lights up with flashes of lightning and I fear for a moment that it's a sign of my impending doom.

Thinking of my mother, I hurry to bed and jump under the covers like a small child and not the fully grown, capable woman I am.

It's going to be a long night.

Sleep doesn't come easily and I toss and turn all night to the sound of the summer storm raging outside.

When I wake, all blurry eyed and exhausted in the morning to the sounds of summer birds singing their praises for the day ahead, I roll over and shriek.

Scurrying backwards, I hit the wall my bed rests against and stare wide eyed at the emerald stone winking at me. The necklace the woman from the path presented to me lays perfectly positioned on my pillow.

Heart in my throat, it takes a great deal of time to process what this means. There is no explanation for how it got in here. Anna isn't in the apartment, it's too early for her, and while she should be here to attend to me in the morning, I let her go. I'd rather be on my own anyway.

I would've heard an intruder with the crappy sleep I got last night and the windows are still firmly locked.

Reaching out slowly, like the necklace might turn into a snake and bite me, I finger the surprisingly warm stone and recoil away from it again. Quickly assessing my rooms once more, I don't see any sign that someone entered my personal space.

Picking up the emerald, I balance it in my palm trying to fight against the words screaming in my head.

There is only one way to save my father and I have the answer.

I just have to find the courage.

CHAPTER SIX

'You are distracted tonight, Lady,' Father Fredrick states from across the table, drawing attention to the fact that I haven't eaten a single thing off my plate since dinner started.

Father Fredrick and Kieran forced me to come to the dining hall this evening for our meal. They like to encourage me to show my face around the castle. The political reasons are lost on me.

I don't want to be here, surrounded by nobles that have their own agendas. Kieran sits to my left and one of Father Fredrick's followers sits to my right. The man is barely an adult and wears the garb of a person who is thinking of following a life of faith and devotion. The other faces at the table are a mixture of off-duty officers who eat with Kieran every night and Father Fredricks friends.

'Sorry,' I reply automatically, pushing my plate away. 'There is a great deal on my mind tonight.'

'Your father will be well, Lady Susyri,' the young man says kindly and I can only smile in return.

That isn't what has my thoughts raging tonight. It's the emerald stone I have safely hidden in my rooms. Since finding it on my pillow, I've replayed the encounter in the garden, over and over. Each time it seems more absurd that I'm entertaining the idea of going.

I can't go on such a quest. There is no way I can survive. No way that I have any sort of chance to meet the Alpha Lord of the Ekalus. They're monsters.

Since I can remember, the stories that I've been told of their predatory nature, their hatred for our kind and their haunting ability to shift their body to resemble a human, has petrified me. Stories say they have razor-sharp teeth and claws for fingers, even when they are in their 'human' skin.

I shudder and nod when Kieran asks if I'm well.

A small commotion at the front of the dining hall draws my attention and has me contemplating my chances of surviving if I stay and my father dies. The Queen is shouting at a servant for not being 'quick enough' and the nobles around her laugh too loudly. The horrible woman laps up the attention. Her gaze slowly moves and before I can avert my eyes, she catches me staring. Instead of getting her usual scowl though, she smirks and I swear it's pure evil.

I turn away only because drawing attention to myself isn't wise right now.

'Do you mind, Lady?' the young acolyte asks me as he indicates to my un-touched plate of food.

'Of course,' I reply, eager to not let anything go to waste. There wasn't a great deal of food set out tonight for some reason and a number of the people at our table seem to still be hungry.

'Thank you,' he responses eagerly and begins to devour my food, leaving me to fall back into the pit of uncertainty in my mind.

It's never-ending. Every thought leads to more questions and reasons why following the instructions to Ekalus Peak is ludicrous. I'm not equipped to go on a quest, on my own.

'Paul, are you well?'

It's the concern in Father Fredrick's words that pull me from my growing anxiety. The young man beside me shakes his head and begins to cough over my plate.

My heartrate spikes as his face reddens to an unnatural colour.

'I think he is choking!' A woman down the table shrieks and I quickly begin to pound on his back.

The sound that comes from the poor man's lips has half the table jump to their feet. Someone shouts for a healer and Kieran grabs my shoulders and pulls me from the table, his large frame half blocking me from the scene as Paul begins to convulse, white foam bubbling from his lips.

Soldiers run over, laying the poor young man on the ground under Father Fredrick's instruction but there is nothing anyone can do.

His body shudders. The noises coming from him are haunting and loud. A woman is screaming. Men shout orders.

I watch in stunned horror as the strange froth dripping down his face is now reddish and brown. Kieran holds me close as if he is worried whatever is happening could hurt me too.

A healer comes racing over and only hovers like he has no idea what to do. Then, nothing.

Paul's body stops shaking. Stops making any noise.

Father Fredrick hangs his head, his hand shaking slightly as he closes the dead boy's eyes. 'He is gone.'

No one speaks. No one moves.

He was fine a moment ago. Until he ate my…I don't know what me has look up and over at the Queen's table and when I do, all I can think is how annoyed she appears. Her grin from earlier is back to her usual scowl and I know that her anger has nothing to do with that fact a man is dead.

Her focus flicks to me once more and she snarls.

I can't help but think that Paul's fate was meant for me.

I race back to my apartment with my heart in my throat and my body trembling.

Slamming the door behind me, I latch it closed and pull over a chair to block the way. I'm probably being silly but I can't shake the fear that Paul was poisoned eating off *my* plate.

Running to the chest of drawers near the window, I grab the small, locked box I've hidden at the back and pull out the emerald necklace.

Staying here or going on this quest doesn't seem like much of a choice anymore. I will die if I stay here and I may die on a road to Ekalus Peak. At least if I take a chance on the Tilman Road there is a small possibility I could save my father.

What do I have to lose anymore?

CHAPTER SEVEN

'I've sent word to the Lord and Lady Highben.'

'What?' I drop the bag I'm filling with supplies and spin on my heels. I woke this morning determined to leave, having made my decision after contemplating my options all night.

Father Fredrick stands in the doorway to my apartment with a grim look on his face. 'Why would you do that?'

Frowning deeply, the aging man shakes his head as if I'm some child who has just asked a silly question. 'Because it's the right thing to do, Susyri.'

'What happened to the family outside the kingdom who agreed to take me in? You said you had friends that could take me.' He doesn't know I will be leaving tonight, yet, I want to know what has changed.

'I agree with Master Kieran. We spoke late into the night after the unfortunate incident with Paul. As I've been granted the right to help you in these matters of betrothal before your father got sick, I reached out to the Highben's. I'm only thinking of your safety, child. The Highben family will be here as soon as they're able.

The news of your acceptance to marry their son will be announced by the end of today and their family name can be used to protect you until they get here.'

Opening and closing my mouth, I find I have nothing to say in reply to that. Here I am, packing, with the plan to leave under the cover of darkness, on a quest that I doubt I'll be able to finish or survive, and now I find out that I'm to marry Lord Hamish Highben. What has my life become? A week ago, I was bored with my existence and was longing for adventure. *What I'd give to go back to that day!*

I sit down slowly on the closest chair, fearing my legs aren't able to keep me upright anymore.

Hands running through the midnight strands I have tied into a high, messy, up-do, I find it hard to control my heartrate. It doesn't matter what I decide now. I'll go on this quest to save my father, to hopefully save myself from death at the hand of the Queen and her lackeys. However, if I don't die on this quest, I will be given to some noble and have my life be over anyway.

It doesn't matter what I do now. I either die or I save the King and then my life is tied to Lord Boring-Old Hamish Highben.

'I wish you'd have spoken to me,' I eventually reply and hear Father Fredrick's boots on the wooden floors.

'It's for the best, child. You'll see that soon enough. You will be well looked after. You'll have a title and a household to manage. A chance at a real life away from this place.'

I want to scream that what I'll really have is a life stuck inside some castle where I'll be expected to pop out sons for the Highben family line.

There is no way my future husband will let me train or walk the estates at night because I love the stars. He won't allow me to go into town and shop at the markets for berries and trinkets, which is my favourite thing to do every market day. I'll be married, producing Highben heirs and ultimately, owned by my husband.

'Susyri, I did what had to be done to save your life.'

I look up at the tone of Father Fredrick's voice and realise that he's genuine in his concern for me.

'I understand,' I whisper, afraid that I'll give away the true extent of my raging emotions if I speak any louder.

Father Fredrick sits down across from me with a sigh. His large hand reaches over the table to grab the one I have clenched against the surface. 'I'm sorry, Susyri. I know that you wanted something more in life but these are the cards you were dealt and the life you were given. We all have our duty and yours is to be the daughter of the King. To marry a lord, give him heirs that have the same blood as the ruling family. The Fire Isles are said to be beautiful and the people both welcoming and kind. You will be happy across the seas. I'm sure of it.'

Nodding, I try to smile my reassurance that I'm okay and I think I do a decent job at pretending because Father Fedrick leaves soon after with a satisfied grin. He informed me that he was heading out to speak to some nobles about the upcoming arrangement and looked pretty happy at the prospect.

I sit at that table for too long, contemplating my situation. I feel like my entire world is crumbling down around me. It's been a handful of days and everything is so uncertain.

I've thought about my death more times in the last two weeks than a woman should at only twenty-three years of age.

Allowing myself a few more moments to wallow in self-pity, I steel my spine, tell myself to get over it, and continue packing for my insane quest before Anna comes to 'help' around the place.

Throwing necessities into my bag, my focus snags on the emerald necklace lying beside some of my garments. I've been finding it hard to not stare at it and eventually pick it up and throw it around my neck, just so that I don't get lost in the colour of it again.

The weight of it surprises me and I suck in a breath at the bite of it against my skin. It burns like a touch of fire and settles to a bearable level just before I go to remove it from my body.

I leave it where it is.

A deep sense of foreboding has me shiver.

This is insanity.

CHAPTER EIGHT

Touching the jewel hanging under my shirt, I try to keep my movements calm and unhurried. The castle grounds are quiet because of the late hour and I take one of the lesser used paths that wraps around the back of the barracks and mess hall to the stable. I've spent all day planning this.

'Lady Susyri?'

Spinning, I flinch at the sight of the woman who appears from behind the building. There's a soldier hanging in the shadows behind her and I nearly roll my eyes.

Anna's scrutinising gaze runs up and down my travel outfit. 'Where are you going?' she demands like she is the Lady and I'm the servant. This woman is a curse.

'I'm clearing my mind, Anna. No need to worry.' I keep my voice as calm and light as possible.

Turning so that she doesn't see the sword strapped to my hip, I wait for her to reply.

One eyebrow rising in of a look of reproach only Anna can achieve, she makes an unsatisfied noise. 'You should be back in your rooms. I hear that Lord Highben likes his young ladies well rested and pretty.' I swear she says 'pretty' like I could never achieve that level of beauty required to marry a Lord like Hamish Highben.

Biting the inside of my mouth to keep my anger in check, I manage to snarl a, 'I'll be sure to rest up just before his arrival. Now, good evening. I will leave you to your—' making a point of looking over her shoulder at the man I know she was sneaking in the shadows with, I finish with, '—fun.'

Turning on my heels, I try not to appear to be hurrying away even though my heart is pounding at my deception and the thought of what I'm doing. I swear I hear her call me a 'bitch' under her breath but I don't care about her words or what she thinks.

Not when I have to get to my horse and out of the stables without anyone seeing and raising the alarm.

Shifts in the stables and on the grounds should be changing in the next few moments and I jog the rest of the way when I know Anna and her *friend* can't see me.

By some miracle, I make it into the stables and retrieve my horse without being noticed. Toppin, my palfrey, is a reliable brown horse who was gifted to me by the King when I 'came-of-age'. It was the most embarrassing moment of my life when he gave it to me. He declared to everyone that I was a fully grown woman in front of the entire court that morning he presented it to me.

I think I was a horrible shade of red the entire week and refused to do anything but lay around in my apartment for the remainder of the month. Things changed dramatically after that.

The Queen took more notice of me, as did most of the nobles. I think the Queen and her 'followers' were hoping I'd just disappear, but when I came-of-age I was no longer able to be ignored.

Toppin seems to sense my need for stealth as he chomps quietly on the apples I feed him to get him to follow through the grounds.

We have to stop a few times and I even fear that I've been caught when one soldier shouts something in the distance.

It's a painfully long and tedious task getting out of the castle grounds and I eventually find myself in the saddle, galloping through the open fields surrounding the castle not believing that I had achieved the impossible. There is also a pounding need to go back to my apartment and not do this. The only thing that keeps me pushing Toppin harder to get away is the knowledge that I'm the daughter of the King. It is my job and duty to try and save him and protect this kingdom from the bitch Queen who will reign over us all if I fail.

CHAPTER NINE

Splashing my face with cold water from the lake, I try to cool myself down before going back to the Tilman Road.

The damn road is haunting my waking and sleeping hours. It's been four days since leaving the castle and all I've done is travel on this relentless strip of dirt, trying not to question every decision I've made so far. The stupidity going on this useless, dangerous journey is not lost on me while I jump back onto Toppin thinking of my mission and why I'm here.

I'm searching for a miracle. For my father. For the entire kingdom. For myself.

I can only imagine what everyone at court is thinking and saying about my disappearance. They're probably gossiping that I ran away in fear or probably that I'm chucking a tantrum about the betrothal.

The thought actually infuriates me. I've spent most of my entire life dealing with the hatred from the Queen and her supporters. The whispers, exclusion and the bullying—it's relentless and constant.

Being a bastard is hard.

My life as a child was filled with laughter and love and lazy days walking the fields with my mother. We had a beautiful estate in the countryside, far from the city, with rolling hills and a small pond. We even had a servant or two. Yes, I found out as I got older that it was all owned by the King and gifted to his mistress, my mother, but when you're young these things don't seem to matter as much.

I didn't understand what it all meant until I was much older. There are days when I hate her for what she did. I hate her for dying and leaving me. For being his mistress and creating me.

I stand tall and lift my face to the sun to feel it's heat and try to expel the painful memories that threaten to consume me.

Touching the jewel securely hidden under my tunic, I still find it unbelievable that I'm doing this. That I'm listening to some stranger about a quest to visit Ekalus Peak. The stone sitting between my breasts is light despite the size of the deep green jewel and there's a warmth that seeps from the emerald that took me a day or so to get used to. Now, I don't think I'd be comfortable if I couldn't feel it. It might be the dangerous journey or the fact that I don't know where I'm going to sleep tonight now that I'm further down the road, but I feel better with it on. Like it's somehow guiding me along this road.

I swear, yesterday when the sun went down quicker than I predicted and I was left riding in the dark afternoon, it glowed slightly, giving me some light to get to an inn safely.

There are small towns along the Tilman Road that I've mapped out. Most are very busy, but I've always found a room to stay in and out of the thin forest that hugs both sides of the road.

I have definitely seen a change in people the further I get on this journey. The last inn wasn't as welcoming.

With a deep sigh, I nudge Toppin to move a little faster, he doesn't seem impressed. I don't blame the poor animal. We're both over this trip already. I'm in desperate need of a bath and would kill for a meal prepared by the castle cooks. I'd give anything for some bread that wasn't stale and ale that didn't taste like someone had made it in their stable.

Cursing the hot sun, I look to the peak in the distance. The mountain that houses the Ekalus shifters. The place where my journey will end, if I don't die along the way, that is.

The mountain looks so small from this far away and Ekalus Peak is many things and small is not one of them. The mountain rises like a beast into the sky. The top puncturing the clouds.

My thoughts are a mess of concerns and prophecies of death.

Reining in my emotions, I keep my focus on one thing at a time. At this point of the quest, I need information on the Dead Forest. I have no idea what or where it is and decide that's my main priority right now.

Fear of impending death can wait until later.

CHAPTER TEN

'Please, I'm just looking for information.'
'You won't get any help from people around here, Miss. So, I say you take a seat, fill your belly, and leave this town quick smart. You shouldn't be in a place like this on your own anyways,' the broad shouldered woman behind the counter tells me in a gravelly tone.

I've been on this trip for seven days now and this is the second town I've ventured into to try and find someone who can help me find the answers I need on the Dead Forest. A forest that doesn't exist on my map or any other that I've ever seen.

Leaning over the stained wood counter a little, I give no mind to the rowdy men and woman around me. It's not even dinner time yet and it seems most of the village is in here having a great time. The food does smell good, and while I really want to eat, I also need someone to speak to me.

'I just need information on the Dead Forest and then I'll be on my way.' An eerie silence falls on the tavern and I look around to see that I'm now the centre of attention.

The woman I was speaking to, who I know is the owner of this inn, places her hands on her round hips with a look that could turn milk sour.

She stomps over and glares right at me.

'You listen here, girl. We don't talk nonsense in these parts and we definitely don't discuss a forest that doesn't exist and is illegal to speak about under the laws of the King. These are dangerous times with the King on his deathbed and I think it best that you leave.' Her full bosom almost pumps into my own chest and I lean back a little.

I wasn't expecting this reaction nor was I aware that speaking about the Dead Forest is illegal.

'I'm sorry,' I stutter. 'I didn't realise what I was asking.'

'Piece of advice for you before you get out of our town. You should always know what you're about to say and the meaning behind your words. Discussing the Tilman Road can get you killed and a pretty little thing like you would be an awful shame to lose to the men that stalk these parts.'

Completely taken aback, I nod once, take one last good look at the woman who is now grinning maliciously at me, and leave.

I make a point of keeping my head down and don't think I take a breath until I jump on my horse and lead him out of this weird place.

Later that night, I sit under a tree with Toppin lying beside me, blocking out some of the wind, while rain covers everything I own. Using his large body for heat, I cuddle with him and apologise over and over for making him come with me.

The poor beast just throws his head from side to side, he's clearly got the shits and I don't blame him. I took him from his lovely home in the most luxurious stables in the kingdom to this damn place.

The road is surrounded by trees on either side and looking at my map again, I realise that this is what I'm in for until I get right to the end. There are multiple towns along the way but after my last encounter I decide to be a bit more selective on what places I'll actually visit. I have no idea what I'm going to do. I need information or this entire quest will be for nothing.

It takes me all night to reassess my plans and then try to get some sleep, which is really just me resting my eyes, praying that I don't die by morning.

CHAPTER ELEVEN

Slowing Toppin down at the sound of metal slamming against metal. I curse the heavens because that sound could mean only one thing—a fight up ahead. A fight I'm going to have to pass.

Last night I barely got any sleep because of the torrential rain and now the sun is hot and I'm all sweaty.

It's disgusting.

Frankly, I have no time for this shit.

I don't want to get involved in anything that doesn't concern me. Yet, here I am, gripping the sword at my hip and cautiously rounding the next bend.

The sight has me stop Toppin. Not because I find it odd that there's a fight on the Tilman Road, I stop for a completely different reason.

The battle up ahead seems to be at an impasse as I take in the scene.

A group of very hairy, very angry looking men, circle a lone figure who stands with his back to me. His long sword pointed to the dirt road.

One against five.

My stupid sense of duty begins to override the voice in my head that tells me to keep going and I sit glued to the spot unsure of what to do.

Swords swinging, the five men attack at once and my mouth drops open when the man at the centre raises his own weapon and moves.

Stepping and slicing, blocking and kicking.

He deflects each attack.

The fact that he's obviously ten times the fighter they are doesn't seem to faze the robbers. Each one takes a blow to the face, the stomach, the side, then they jump away to let their friend take over the assault.

I know what they're doing. I have studied battle strategy since I was an adolescent, the attackers are using a tactic to wear out their opponent. I will give it to them, they're determined to win even though the single man, with his broad shoulders and muscular, thick arms, handles himself like a true warrior.

I sit watching him move for longer than is appropriate and despite the ache in my chest to go over there, I decide to mind my own business.

Kicking my horse towards the trees with the intent to go around the road, we begin to move, until a small grunt of pain catches my attention. The sound overtakes my senses and has my gaze fly to the altercation once more. A force outside of my body screams at me to assist and I curse loudly at my stupidity, jump from Toppin and draw my weapon.

I have no idea what or why I'm doing this.

Advancing toward the group, I read the situation with the precision of a fighter trained by one of the best swordsmen in the kingdom. Kieran's words fill my mind and as if he was standing beside me, I nod at the instructions he gives.

I take advantage of the fact that none of the attackers have noticed me yet.

The group have the man still within their circle and the poor victim seems to have been hurt. Very aware of what's going on, I realise that the guy favours his left side as he side-steps the next man who comes for him with a dagger.

With a deep breath, I block the blade intended to stab the single man in the back, with my sword.

The impact vibrates up my arm.

Dropping low, I dive up and into the chest of the hairy robber, making the oversized brute stumble backward.

His eyes widen and unable to get his feet under himself, he falls heavily to the ground with a thud.

I don't pay him any more attention as I throw myself into the fight.

CHAPTER TWELVE

Brushing the dirt off my pants, I grab the skin of water from my saddlebag and keep one eye on the man who busies himself with stealing from the immobile men on the floor.

Heart pounding for some nameless reason, I take the time to admire the view, because my word, he is *stunning*. His carved body seems to be made of stone as I watch him bend and rob the guy I stabbed towards the end of the fight.

It's not just the muscles I can see straining under his tunic and pants, or the hand crafted features of his face that has me unable to look away. I have seen beauty before, but this is different. There is something about him. Something about his eyes that captivate me.

When the battle was won and he finally looked down at me, his deep ever-green eyes seemed to look straight into my soul. The colour so striking and peculiar that I actually gasped when our gazes locked.

Remembering how it all made me feel, my hand goes to the necklace tucked under my tunic.

For some reason, his eyes make me think of the emerald necklace around my neck. I swear I even felt the stone heat against my skin. It felt as if it burnt me with a sizzling kiss.

We stared for a few heartbeats after our victory. He towered over me, my head coming to his broad, defined chest. The man's beauty was so striking that I had to fight my reflexes to not step back from the energy that surrounded him.

I rub my hand up and down my arm at the memory of how my skin prickled under his assessment.

Unable to not stare from the safety of my horse, I try to understand what has me so mesmerised and unwilling to leave without speaking to him first.

His face is all masculine lines. The soft brown, shoulder length hair that has been tied up, haphazardly at his nape appears silky smooth. His straight nose and cheekbones looked to be made of marble. Yet all I can think of is that I've never, ever, seen eyes so bright and captivating.

There was a voice in my head that whispered for me to run while I stood gaping like a fool up at him with the bodies of his attackers surrounding us.

The battle was won quickly and I stood there like an idiot waiting for him to say something. However, all I got was a glare. His eyes skimming over me like he was disgusted to have the assistance of a woman, and then he walked away.

No word of thanks.

Nothing.

I stormed over to Toppin once everything settled and practically stomped my feet around like a child having a tantrum at the fact that he hadn't shown any gratitude for what I did for him.

He'd be dead right now if I hadn't stepped in.

Fucking men.

If I too had a dick, he may have asked me my name, showered me with thanks, and maybe even offered me some food. He probably would've asked to share a fire tonight seeing as how the sun is going down and sticking together would be the smart and logical thing to do.

But no.

I get silence and now he's ignoring me.

Shaking my head from the damn un-lady like thoughts intruding into my mind about sharing a fire and the night with him, I finally look away and return to my saddle.

'You're welcome for saving you, by the way,' I call to the un-grateful ass I just helped.

The infuriating prick keeps his back turned, totally snubbing me. He just continues doing whatever he's doing.

Stealing and robbing the robbers, I guess.

Mumbling an array of various colourful cuss words, I continue on my journey, not bothering to look back.

CHAPTER THIRTEEN

For three days I travel in the heat and rain, miserable and regretting every decision I've made so far. I've even attempted heading into towns and asking for information on the Dead Forest multiple times.

In the first town, I got the cold shoulder. The second, I was told to take my black magic talk with me to the pits of hell—which I thought was very dramatic. The third place told me to leave and never come back.

So, as I ride up to the larger town of Greceton, I'm exhausted and feeling as if I'll never find any answers to help me plan what I'm going to do when this road ends.

It's late afternoon by the time I get Toppin into a stable for the night and find the tavern, which really isn't that hard to miss. The large square in the centre of town is busy and everyone seems to be spilling out of the building to the left.

The tavern's wooden walls and wide, swinging doors are bright with light and sounds. A beacon, promising warmth and food. It draws me to it.

Trying to stay as inconspicuous as possible, I keep my hood over my head and my saddlebag on my back.

I make my way through the crowded space, a little disorientated by the noise, and stop at the long, stained bar.

There are three men behind the counter, all busy working and laughing with their patrons. There are a few groups standing around with weapons strapped to their hips. Everyone in this place gives off 'don't mess with me' vibes and I really have no desire to piss anyone off. So, I wait at the counter until the man, I'm guessing is the tavern owner, notices me.

'Take a seat Miss, and if you'd be wanting a room, you'll need to tell me now as it's a busy night and we're nearly booked,' the middle-aged tavern owner shouts while filling two jugs of some bubbly liquid that I don't think is beer.

'I'd actually like to ask for some assistance, I'm looking for some information.' I keep a watchful eye on the patrons standing around to make sure no one is listening, which is hard with how many people are here.

The owner just raises a brow and comes over to stand directly in front of me. His gaze travels over my outfit and over my shoulder. 'You alone?'

'That isn't your concern, Sir,' I respond as politely as possible and only because he doesn't seem creepy, more like trying to work me out. He doesn't respond and I know I've given away a great deal of information about myself.

I sound like a noble.

He raises that same eyebrow again and nods. 'What information you looking for?'

'I need information about the Dead Forest.' I don't know what makes me shiver or what causes the strange feeling that prickles the back of my neck. I look over my shoulder quickly to make sure no one's standing behind me. After what happened in that last tavern, I don't want to cause a scene again.

The tavern owner tilts his head as if thinking through his response. 'There's no such place.'

'I know.' I dig in my back pocket and pull out three silver pieces, having come to the conclusion last night that I need to use money to entice some help. 'This should be enough for a meal and some ale.' I place the money on the counter knowing it's more than enough for what I'm asking, and he seems to know it.

Smiling wide, he shows off his two missing front teeth and nods. 'Take a seat and I'll get a server to bring you food soon.'

A little relieved that I wasn't run out of town again, I choose a table tucked into the back corner and wait a while.

Quicker than I expect, a stone-faced server drops a bowl of stew and a mug of ale in front of me. I watch as he walks away without a word and start to eat the bland plate of food. It's gross but hot and full of vegetables, so I eat it. Anything is better than dried meat and three-day-old bread.

Trying to keep my thoughts away from questioning what kind of meat I'm eating, I shovel it into my mouth. On a quest like this, I feel I need to count my blessings because only the heavens know if there will be a chance to eat like this tomorrow.

Belly filling up, I slow down and try to savour my bites and try the bread, which is surprisingly good.

The tavern is warm and loud. Laughter and shouting is drowned out by more laughing and shouting. I do my best to stay hidden in my corner, however, I can feel eyes on me and I chance a glance around the large room. Heart pumping at the small smirk I receive from a number of shady men sitting around the space, I pull the hood on my small cape down lower and check that my weapon is still close on my hip.

That's when I hear the group behind me. My blood runs cold at their words. 'They say she ran away and the Queen is looking for her.' *Her. Me?*

I keep my focus on my food.

'Heard there's a massive reward for finding her.'

'Dead or alive.' The laughter makes me sick to my stomach.

It has to be me.

'Will be pretty hard to work out who the run-away bastard is though. Has anyone outside of the court even seen her?' the first voice says and I try really hard not to vomit everywhere.

I know I should leave but I have no other options. I have to hold onto the hope that I might get some answers of where the Dead Forest is. However, the owner I spoke to is behind the bar again, filling orders. So I guess I'll be waiting all night, which puts me in a precarious situation.

Leave and get lost when this damn road ends or stay and draw attention.

My options are minimal.

CHAPTER FOURTEEN

Too lost in thought, I almost jump out of my skin when a figure drops heavily into the chair across from me. On instinct, I pull the dagger from my belt. My heart races and then calms when ever-green eyes stare back at me. Grabbing at my bowl of stew, the man from the road pulls it towards himself and begins to dig in, totally unconcerned with the knife I'm holding or the look on my face. *Or* the fact that he's eating *my* food.

'Go right ahead,' I huff, sheathing my weapon and taking a shaking drink of ale. His grunt of recognition ignites a rage inside my blood that has me snap, 'you're welcome. Again!'

I watch him spoon large mouthfuls of stew into his mouth and honestly it shouldn't make my thighs clench or my skin feel too tight but it does. I think of that mouth and being that spoon and then kick myself for being a moron. I put my odd behaviour down to the fact that it's been a long and lonely week on the road and not because the sight of this gorgeous man does some weird and wonderful things to my insides.

We sit in silence. Me drinking and watching him like a stalker, and him eating like he hasn't in months.

I get so accustomed to the silence that I jump when he speaks. 'You do realise that you're not safe sitting in this tavern alone, yes?'

It takes my mind a good minute before I'm able to respond. The look he gives me knocks the air from my lungs and I begin to question the sanity of the robbers who dared try to fight this man.

He's huge and imposing. His voice is deep and oddly musical.

It promises death and pleasure.

Destruction and euphoria.

I realise that I could listen to it for days and never get used to the low timbre, the distinctly masculine depth.

I clear my throat and find my composure. 'I'm perfectly fine, thank you.'

Downing the remainder of *my* drink, he continues, 'you're a girl. Shouldn't you be at home sewing or cooking or something? Isn't that what girls like you do?'

Did he... 'Excuse me? Girls like me?' What does that even mean? I growl a noise I've never made before and those ever-green eyes seem to light up. I have an overwhelming need to smack him. 'Firstly, I *am* a girl. I do not cook or sew. And, if I wanted to cook and sew, then that is what I would be doing right now. Secondly, I was the one who saved *you* on the road, remember? I can take care of myself just fine as you well know!' I can feel the heat rising to my cheeks in outrage. I have to stop my hand from drawing my dagger again.

His musical laughter causes everyone in the tavern to look towards our dark corner. My heart responds to the sound and I truly hate myself.

He just continues to laugh while I contemplate if he's drunk.

Coming to the conclusion that he is, I eye the still busy tavern owner, ignoring my guest completely.

'You waiting for something?'

'What's that to you?' I snap, my focus on the man serving a new table of very rough looking men. I watch as he exchanges one of my silver coins with the extra scary looking one.

Averting my eyes quickly when the tavern owner points in my direction, I don't miss the way the man pocketing my coin looks over.

'I hope you know what you're doing.'

Blinking back up at the strange man eating my meal, I touch the stone under my tunic as that strange warmth sizzles against my skin. Ever-Green Eyes frowns, his focus on my hand and I watch as they travel back to my face.

'What do you mean?' I question, my voice wobbling a little.

I watch as he gives me a *don't be dumb* kind of look before he rises. His eyes darken. 'Watch your back girl, this road is not a safe place to be on your own,' is all he says before he walks away and disappears in the crowded tavern.

CHAPTER FIFTEEN

'What is this?' I ask, not daring to touch what appears to be a stained rolled cloth with something heavy inside it.

The tavern owner grunts that it's what I was looking for. 'Don't open it here. Your room upstairs is ready for the night,' he says before walking away without a backwards glance.

It takes a moment to understand what he's just said. 'I didn't book a room,' I shout after him.

'It was booked for you! Room Three, up the stairs,' he shouts back over his shoulder and disappears.

Totally confused, I hurriedly collect my things. My mind only thinking of a warm bed and hot water. I head towards the stairs along the back wall and to the first floor. The lights are dim and I stare down the long corridor, unsure why my instincts are screaming at me to think through what I'm doing.

Fuelled by my desire to not sleep outside, I pass the first two doors and open the door with the '3' on it. It swings open with a creak.

Still a little uncertain, I search the space around the double bed, trying to not look too closely at the blankets. There's a small bathroom connected to the room that is about five steps wide with a tiny shower. Nothing fancy, and yet, the elation I feel at not being out in the forest tonight has me do a little happy dance before I throw my bag down and sit on the end of the squeaky mattress.

Pulling out the wrapped cloth the tavern owner gave me, I carefully unfold it and study the scroll that drops onto my lap. The very worn, thick paper shakes in my hands as I lift it up and unfold it over the surface of the bed.

I nearly shout at the sheer joy of what I've acquired. It's a map of the kingdom. Though this map is nothing like any I've ever studied before. It's only recognisable from the location of the cities and towns at the top of the paper to the peak at the bottom, everything else in between is a circus of lines and squiggles.

Tracing a finger over the road I am on, I watch it divide at its end.

One path leads to more small towns, and the other... *the Dead Forest.*

I can't believe that I've never seen or heard of a forest that spans a good distance of the map. Finger still following the lines on the parchment, I curse the fact that both paths at the end of the Tilman Road seem to lead to Ekalus Peak.

This is it. This is what I needed.

There are no towns and no roads within the Dead Forest and while I'm so happy I could shout in joy, I'm also concerned and afraid of what is ahead of me.

I study the map until I can't keep my eyes open any longer.

Placing it back as carefully as I can, I secure my bag and make sure that the door to the hallway is locked. I'm not sure how effective it will be keeping anyone out so I pull the chair in the corner over to try and block it. Might not do much, but it will alert me if someone tries to break in, hopefully.

Knowing it's the best I can do, I head into the bathroom and try to wash some of the road off me.

I don't know what wakes me.

I blink my eyes open and process where I am. Having slept in my travel pants and tunic, I sit up on my elbows and try to understand what has my instincts screaming at me to be alert.

That's when I finally hear it, my focus snaps to the door and I watch as a shadow moves under the gap of it. It's the middle of the night and the tavern below is completely quiet. Meaning that no one should be hanging around in the hallway. Unless they're up to no good.

Holding my breath, I listen and watch as the doorknob is tested. The *squeak* has me jump silently off the bed, taking the dagger under my pillow with me.

Fear pumping through my veins, I listen to the squeak again and quickly throw on my warm cape and pull my bag onto my back as quietly as I can. I guess about three sets of heavy boots outside.

Creeping to the window, I open it and begin to climb out. I'd already worked out a few options if I was ambushed tonight before I fell asleep. I learnt that in numerous lessons with Kieran over the years.

Trying to be quiet, I slip out into the night and shimmy down the drainpipes with only the light from the moon guiding me.

Heart pounding, my blood rushes violently in my veins. I slip just a few feet from the ground and slam into the hard floor beside the back of the tavern with a thud.

On my butt and a little winded, I push myself up and try to keep my head. There isn't a soul in sight. A good and bad thing. No one to help and no one out here to worry about. At least not yet.

Pushing myself against the side of the building, I take a moment to catch my breath. I see the trees around the town, some dwellings in the distance. The stable is over to the right.

Following the building on soft steps, I peek around the corner to see if there's anyone hanging around.

There's a small group of hooded figures standing near their horses. I don't know how I know but I'm fairly certain they're with the ones that were trying to get into my rooms.

Trying to work out a plan of attack, I don't hear the person who comes up behind me until I'm grabbed roughly and slammed, back-first, into the hard, dirt floor with a shriek of pain and shock.

CHAPTER SIXTEEN

I fight with everything I have in me. My arms swing and my nails scratch at the face of the man on top of me, pinning me to the ground. His heavy weight is almost impossible to breathe under, the smell of him isn't helping either. Smacking him up the side of the face, I'm gifted my own hit that has me seeing stars.

Screaming and shouting for him to let me go, I can feel the other men standing around watching. Some laugh. Others jeer at how they have 'found me'. The other comments are foul and terrifying, their plans of what they want to do to me shocks me to my core.

In that moment, I realise I've lived a very sheltered life.

I remember their voices from earlier in the tavern, they're the ones that were speaking about the bounty on my head. Dead or alive. That is what they said.

I don't give the man a chance to grab at my arms and yet, I'm powerless when two others grip my wrists and pull them on either side of my head, keeping me from fighting back.

'Looks like we bagged a princess,' the one near my head says.

'Let me go!'

More laughter. Every hair on my body stand on end.

The man lying on me runs his creepy black eyes over my body and I watch in horror as they land on my throat. I panic. His gross, dirt covered hand comes up to grip the chain around my neck and I panic because the emerald must have slipped out from under my tunic.

'What's this?' he asks. He grins and I swallow bile at the sight of his black-stained teeth. His face lights up and I struggle harder. I hate his hands that close to my chest.

He doesn't take the necklace off me or touch the stone itself, just studies it, like he knows he has found a massive prize.

'We should ask for double the reward,' someone behind me announces. 'Tell 'em we'll throw in the expensive jewel.'

'Maybe it belongs to the King. They'll want it back,' another one says.

'Check to see if the map is in her bag.' There are so many voices that I have no idea how many men are watching.

'She doesn't need to be alive.'

I scream again, this time in anger for being so helpless. I can't stand it.

'We'll have a taste first? All of us can take turns.'

The smelly guy on top of me makes all sorts of disgusting comments. He drops the necklace which has the stone smack into my clavicle, it feels like it's on fire.

Bucking in a useless attempt to get free, I watch in horror as his face falls to my neck and I feel his tongue on my skin. I gag and then turn my head and scream in his ear.

Like, all-out shriek, in the way that Kieran taught me in my defence training, right in his ear.

The man curses and reels back. Then he is gone. His entire body is pulled off me. Before I can register the absence of his weight, my hands are free and I'm left blinking up at the massive figure who has two of my assailants in each hand. Holding them up off the ground like they weigh nothing, my saviour laughs joyously as he slams the two men together in a sound that has me flinch.

The pair crumple to the floor and it appears to be the funniest thing that Ever-Green has ever done.

I hear men scream and hooves slamming on the ground as I'm sure most of the others have run away in fear of the mighty male defending me. Ever-Green takes care of two more attackers before I'm able to sit up slowly and look around the quiet town.

Shaking, I take in the unmoving bodies on the ground and the almost peacefulness of the night. Gaze travel up to the man who just saved me from only the heavens know what kind of fate, I find myself unable to communicate properly. All I do is stare.

Ever-Green grins at the carnage and then *walks away*.

He doesn't look back. Doesn't acknowledge my existence. Just raises his hand in the air and then says happily, 'you're welcome!' and disappears behind the tavern like he hasn't a care in the world.

CHAPTER SEVENTEEN

The moon slowly creeps higher as Toppin and I travel quietly on the empty road. I still have no idea what actually happened back there and my cheek is burning from where I was slapped.

I think I'm in shock.

I don't feel scared or sad or even angry anymore. I feel nothing.

The stars twinkle overhead and my thoughts aren't being kind tonight. All I can think about is my father, my messed up life and my dead mother. There are times where I wish for the innocence of youth. When I was a child, I was shielded from the politics of birth and lineage and jealousy. For months, my mother would leave me with my maid and the servants of the house to visit someone. I found out just before her death that she was seeing the King.

As an adult, I can't imagine what drove her to become a mistress. The idea is confusing, and wrong. I try not to judge. It's hard to think that she didn't know what this would do to me. How this would place a target on her daughter's back. How lonely that would make my life.

I have no friends besides two old men who are mostly just bossy advisers. Love will never be on the cards for me and I'll be married soon enough to Lord Hamish Highben and I'll be alone, like I am now, for the rest of my life.

I've known since I was ten that the Queen would do everything in her power to get rid of me. Yet, experiencing it tonight, first-hand, is an entirely different thing. *Was I really that naive?*

To know something and to experience something are two different things. I've never had anyone assault me like that. I realise how much of a sheltered life I've lived and how dumb I was to stay at the tavern when I didn't know who booked me the room. I think in a way I thought the man with the ever-green eyes did, which shouldn't be enough to make me trust anyone. I'm smarter than this.

Hand unconsciously going to the warm jewel around my neck, I press against it as if seeking the comfort of its heat.

That thought is what has the tears eventually start running down my face.

Once they start, I have no control over how fast they fall. Emotions roll through me. One after the other. Anger. Grief. Fear. Frustration. Loneliness. They are all just as painful as the other.

Toppin leads the way and I fall apart on his back. My mind replays everything that happened, from the moment I entered the tavern to the moment I was left on my arse surrounded by bleeding bodies.

When Ever-Green disappeared, I checked to see who was dead and alive. I also made sure I still had the map, which was in my bag, and took a few extra weapons like some kind of Tilman Road robber.

I didn't see a single person when I collected Toppin in a rush and high-tailed it so fast out of that damn town that I'm sure I left something behind.

I can still feel that man's tongue on my neck.

My entire body shakes with each violent sob and I lay my head down on Toppin's neck and hug my horse, not sure if I have the courage and the strength to do this.

CHAPTER EIGHTEEN

I stay out of towns and hardly sleep for three days.

When I do rest, it's with Toppin beside me and a small fire. Every spot I choose is well thought out and if I see travellers, I hide and stay off the road.

The only reason I lead Toppin into the next large town of Dandila is because I run out of food and I need supplies.

I regret it instantly when I pass the first row of buildings. The village is laid out in a massive circle and the realisation that market day is on makes me pause. Anxiety hits pretty hard and I swallow my trepidation at the row of stalls and the sight of shoppers walking in groups as they enjoy the day. Women hold baskets, men drink as they follow along and children run around causing trouble.

I find a spot for Toppin amongst a row of tied horses and make sure he is secure and safe before heading toward the markets in search of some food.

The town is the biggest one I've been to so far and the noise, coupled with the crowd, makes it a little easier to feel like just another person going about their business.

After a few tense moments of looking around and making sure no one is following, I relax and eventually start to enjoy my morning.

The markets have been set up in a kind of organised chaos and the smells lull me into a sense of comfort.

I practically fall over myself at the sight of a fruit merchant and nearly cry at the sight of fresh produce.

The day is surprisingly great. I've had amazing conversations with the locals and my bag is full of supplies, including treats that I'll have a hard time rationing. Let's be honest, I've already eaten half the snacks before getting to the end of the row of first stalls.

Sugary fingers diving back into the small paper bag of baked goods I grabbed at the last shop, I stuff my face and move through the crowd lazily. There are people everywhere. There's a group of young children running ahead of me and I watch suspiciously at the two in the front who are weaving in and out of the crowd. Their grubby hands dive into the back pocket of men and into baskets at women's hips.

Not sure what to do or say, I'm a little shocked that no one seems to be paying these little thieves any attention. I don't know if I should clap them or run over and reprimand their behaviour.

Unclipping my coin purse from my belt, I bring it up and tuck it between my breasts and clutch my bag of pastries like I'm more afraid that someone is going to steal these treats off me.

Nearly choking on my mouthful of sugary greatness, I recognise the thick, muscular back of the man up ahead—their next target.

His white linen tunic is the same as the one he wore when I first saw him on the road. My hand comes up to caress the emerald around my neck. Then clap it over my mouth when I snort in laughter at the little fingers that slip into the purse at Ever-Green's back.

Shoving another pastry into my mouth, I grin and actually spit sugar when another child shows up behind Ever-Green and gets his little fingers into the same purse. By the look of the thing, it's as thick as Ever-Green's arms. And these kids know it.

Walking slowly, I enjoy for a little longer but then decide that I can't call myself a member of the King's court if I don't intervene. He did save my life the other day.

Still trying to keep my joy in check, I intercept the next little robber by grabbing his wrist just before it dives into the purse again.

The child's small squeal has Ever-Green spin with a growl. 'What in the hell?'

I'm crouched down now, looking the small child in the eye. I wonder for a moment what kind of life he has to be so young and doing something that could get him into a great deal of trouble. Stealing in the kingdom is a punishable offense.

Big, round brown eyes stare at me. 'No more,' I say as firmly as I can whilst still being kind.

'Were you stealing from me?' Ever-Green shouts and the poor kid flinches. I can almost taste his fear. I can't blame him, even I feel my skin prickle at the commanding voice that demands he explain what he 'thinks he is doing'.

Having already grabbed a piece of silver from the bag between my breasts, I push it into the young boys hand and tell him to take his friends and find some food. 'Go.'

He runs off and I finally look up at the man looming over me, his brow furrowed at whatever he sees on my face.

Rising, I pop another pastry into my mouth knowing full well that Ever-Green is watching my every move. Eyes locked with his, I grin, not caring that I'm covered in sugar. 'You're welcome.'

I walk away to find some more treats, feeling satisfied and happier than I have in days.

CHAPTER NINETEEN

It's late afternoon and I don't want to get back on the road, so I venture into the tavern at the end of the town for some dinner.

I order way too much food and find a quiet table along the side wall to stuff my face. The place is warm and lively and I feel at ease, which helps me to relax and enjoy my meal.

'They are all legitimate. Every last one. Heart-stones from Ekalus Peak.'

'Move along, old man,' the man at the table not far from mine demands while his friends all laugh and cheer at the merchant whose holding out a fabric looking tray of what appears to be coloured jewels. I can't really see from my seat but they're making enough noise that I can hear every single word of their conversation.

I don't blame the groups that tell the elderly man to keep moving. The merchant is declaring his stones as heart-stones and there's no way in any situation a heart-stone would be here in this town amongst humans. It makes me chuckle just thinking about it.

He clearly needs a new sales strategy. No one in their right mind would believe such a tale, let alone buy something like that.

Even with my belly protesting the amount of sweets I've eaten today, I keep shovelling mouthfuls of delicious meat pie into my mouth. I haven't stopped eating since I got to this town. Three days on the road eating my meagre supplies has made me appreciate the finer things in life, like a fork and a table.

I was so apprehensive this morning about going into public after what happened, and yet, I've had a very enjoyable day. I don't feel uncomfortable and with the place buzzing with people, I know no one is paying any attention to me.

Market days are always grand events no matter where you are in the kingdom. Back home, the city is filled with newcomers and merchants. Food. Wine. Ale. Clothes. Performers. It's my favourite day of the week.

'For you miss, a beautiful heart-stone to hold the heart of an Ekalus.'

I blink at the necklace now dangling in front of me and place down my spoon. The purple gem is pretty, and while it looks nice, I know for a fact that it is a mediocre piece.

'No, thank you,' I say as politely as I can.

The elderly man has salt and pepper hair. His brown overcoat looks way too heavy and his long beard is sticking out all over the place. He doesn't move away, even when I go back to my food.

'A heart-stone is a sacred possession. It's said that each Ekalus has a stone given to them when they come of age and if you find one and wear it around your neck then that Ekalus will do your bidding.

You can command he love you for eternity or kill your enemies. You could even make him buy you more jewels.'

Eyebrow rising at his explanation, I shake my head and fight the need to touch the real stone around my own neck. Why would anyone want to control another being like that? Who would want the love and devotion of a winged demon?

'No,' I say a little more forcefully this time. 'Thank you.' Again, I keep spooning more food into my mouth, giving what I believe, is a clear hint that I'm not interested. However, this man doesn't seem to get the message.

'A pretty girl like you could have the love of an Ekalus easily. All it takes is a stone like this one. You wear it and the Ekalus it's attached to will give you his or her heart.'

Getting a little over this entire conversation and the fact that this man clearly doesn't know what 'no' means, I'm about to tell him that he needs to move on to another table when the chair across from mine is pulled out. The wood scraps along the floor and then creaks when Ever-Green plonks his heavy weight down onto it.

I fight the need to roll my eyes at the sight of him. 'I'm having a good day today so I really don't have the time for you.'

He laughs a deep, musical sound. I'm about to tell him to go away but have just realised that the merchant has stepped back from my table, taking his necklaces with him. So, I shut my mouth. I'd rather the big, grumpy warrior dude than the seedy merchant any day.

Ever-Green studies me as if suspicious of why I've stopped talking. I just focus on eating my delicious meal before it gets cold.

Brow narrowed, he watches the nervous merchant standing there looking all awkward and unsure if he can make this sale now. 'You can go.' Ever-Green dismisses the man so casually that I have to stop chewing the chunk of bread in my mouth to make sure I've heard him correctly.

'Sir, I have a number of lovely pieces for your beautiful wife, here—' The merchant shuts his mouth when Ever-Green's laughter fills the tavern once more.

That sound sets me on fire.

It hurts.

It burns.

It feels so good.

Without much thought, I clutch the heavy jewel around my neck.

'You're wrong, in so many ways.' Ever-Green chuckles while picking up *my* ale and taking a decent swig.

Throwing my hands up in exasperation, I'm totally ignored as he continues to tell the merchant that I'm not his wife, like it's some kind of afront to nature, and then goes on to educate him on heart-stones. 'They aren't given to anyone. An Ekalus earns their heart-stone and that stone will only go to their mate. They aren't something used to control an Ekalus. And never would you just find a heart-stone sitting around. And never would you be able to pick one up like any other stone, unless you are that Ekalus' true love. It would hurt you. Bite. Burn. Sting. Poison. Kill. Whatever.'

Food forgotten, I watch the attractive, definitely drunk man across from me as he lectures us all on heart-stones.

The merchant opens and closes his mouth, listening to Ever-Green's lesson on Ekalus lore.

It's kinda funny.

'Now, we're not interested. Thank you. You can go.' And the merchant listens.

A little annoyed and not particularly surprised that a man would listen to another man more than a young woman, I forget about my food. 'Well, if I thought giving some kind of long-winded lesson in Ekalus lore would get him to leave, I would've started one when he came to the table.'

We sit, staring, neither speaking, until his gaze falls to my pie and back up. That's when I realise that he's waiting for something.

With a sigh, I push my plate over and reclaim my ale. 'You know, I saw your coin purse earlier in the market. I know you can buy your own food.'

Ever-Green just says, 'you're welcome.'

'For what?' I demand, remembering how attractive he is when he eats.

Never in my life have I ever thought I'd find someone's mouth and lips so mesmerising.

It makes me think things I never thought about before.

Like how those lips would feel on mine and what kind of pleasure that mouth could give.

His low timbre voice pulls me out of my inappropriate thoughts. 'For getting that crook away from you. Now, we're even.'

It takes me a moment to understand what he's said. 'Even? No we're not.' *You've got to be kidding me.* 'I stopped pick-pocketers from stealing from you. I saved you on the road, you saved me at...' I can't even finish my sentence without almost gagging. 'I stopped you from losing all your money. Getting a merchant to leave isn't comparable.' Smugly, I sit back in my seat, knowing I'm in the lead.

Ever-Green just keeps eating like I've not spoken. I actually don't think he's listening until he says, 'you stopped them after watching them steal from me three times. We're even.'

Pursing my lips, I don't know if I'm stopping myself from laughing or protesting. He has a point.

He's also completely demolished my pie.

Instead of responding, I stand and hold out my hand. Ever-Green watches it like it's some kind of dangerous beast. 'I'm getting another plate of food and a new ale. This round is on you, so hand some of those coins over.'

The arrogant male huffs and yet still digs around his hip and passes over a few coins.

Grinning my thanks, I leave the table with a swagger in my step, feeling like I've won some kind of big battle.

When I get back from ordering more food, Ever-Green is gone and my plate and ale are both finished.

It just makes me smile.

CHAPTER TWENTY

Something's off.

Standing on the side of the road with Toppin grazing on the small strip of grass, I look out at the row of trees trying to decipher what has changed in the last day and a half of travelling. I stopped to check the map for the hundredth time. The thing is practically permanently attached to my hand at this point. I've slept with it strapped to my chest.

The fabric that holds my breasts in place is now my new bag. After the last town, I keep my map and coin purse in there. I feel I should invent some kind of new fashion piece that does multiple jobs.

Double checking that I haven't made a mistake and turned down the wrong path at some point, I frown, knowing that I'm on the right track. While I'm glad, I'm also really confused. It's been nearly two weeks of the same road and the same environment of tall, skinny trees all lined up in perfect rows. Yet, the world has appeared to have darkened despite the hour and the trees aren't the same here. They're thicker. More clustered together. More fuller and ominous looking. Instead of the bright greens, everything is deeper in colour. Full of vines.

Using all my senses, I notice the lack of sound next. Typically, I'd be hearing birds and animals. Now I just hear...nothing. I think out of everything, that's the part that's freaking me out the most.

With my imagination on overdrive, I push the possibility that I'm looking at growing fog in the distance and red eyes of monsters staring at me from between the trees.

Hopping back in the saddle, I urge Toppin to move faster.

Every so often, my instincts scream at me to double check I'm not being stalked by some Tilman Road beast and decide that the next town will be where we stop tonight.

I regret my decision the moment I enter the next town and get the same uneasy feeling. The darkness seems to have extended into this place and eaten it alive. Toppin's hooves clap against the cracked cobblestones which is odd on so many levels.

Every town I have sought shelter in so far has been dirt tracks and gravel. This one looks to have been built with some love and care and yet, the maintenance is questionable. It's as if in the past it was a lively place, filled with wealth. Now, it's decrepit and creepy.

Dwellings are dotted around the town. There are barns with animals in sight and a few chimneys have smoke spilling out of them.

The same thick forest surrounds the perimeter of the town and when I eventually find the big buildings in the centre and identify the one that must be the inn.

I hesitate.

There should be sound coming from the doors. There should be voices and laughter and the smell of cooking meat. However, there's only silence. After everything I've been through so far on this quest and with all that has happened, I've learnt to listen to my gut.

With a muffled curse under my breath, I stay in my seat and steer Toppin back onto the road.

I have no idea what I should do or where I should stay for the night but here in this creepy village is not it.

CHAPTER TWENTY ONE

There's an unusual chill in the air and I keep Toppin close. I picked a small little clearing just outside of creepy town and have tethered Toppin to the tree at my back so that I can use some of his warmth. The tiny fire I built up is pretty pathetic and is more to chase the darkness away than actually provide any kind of heat.

With the idea of sleeping while out here in the open gives me hives, I pull out the map and study it again. I'm making good progress on the road. The Dead Forest is coming up fast, and looking around, I have a deep, uneasy feeling that I may be glimpsing my fate when I actually get there.

Tonight though, the Dead Forest doesn't have my full attention. It's the peak that sits on the other side of it that has me contemplating my life choices.

Ekalus Peak.

There are multiple mountains behind the main peak, all said to house different colonies of Ekalus. There is only one Alpha Lord though. The Ekalus supreme ruler. The idea of a supreme ruler of those monsters is terrifying. I heard one song where the minstrels sang of the beauty of an Ekalus. I was captivated when he sang of the way they fly, fight and, even though Father Fredrick made me leave the hall when the song changed, how they loved. It made me blush. Hearing how the demons can shift their form from human to winged beasts made my heart race.

Humans are fascinated by them even if we're completely terrified of the idea of seeing one. We know that they exist and we love to listen to songs but we would never want to actually see one. I guess the scariest thing is that they could be walking amongst us and we wouldn't even know, or so the tales go. It doesn't really make much sense.

It's said that once, long ago, humans and Ekalus had a more harmonious relationship. Ekalus moved freely amongst humans, and humans worshipped them. There are songs of great friendships and loves between the two races that are sung on special occasions. It wasn't until the war of the Ekalus which broke out a few hundred years ago that everything fell apart. The war brought death and destruction to the human race. We were caught in the cross-fire, used as pawns in their games. If the stories are true, humans eventually took up arms to retaliate and put an end to the Ekalus power here on earth.

I don't know how it ended with us down here and them up on their peaks. From what I've learnt in my studies, Ekalus are predators. Entire villages have been decimated because of them. I heard once that they eat our souls.

Some say that we are used as sacrifices in their rituals and why every few years there are a string of deaths caused by the terrible monsters.

Fear sits heavy on my chest as I contemplate the ending of this quest. Asking the Alpha Lord for his blood to save my father seems like a sick, unrealistic joke. And I'm the fool who listened to that crazy woman and followed her instructions.

I'm so lost in my own head, wrapped up in rage at my circumstances, that the world slips away. Until the nickering of my horse draws me from my self-deprecating thoughts.

I scan the darkness. My heart quickens for some nameless reason and I place the map back into the bag beside me, slowly and without any sudden movements. The air seems too still and it's why I reach for the sword beside my hip.

Not taking my focus from the trees, I lift my sword, knowing somehow that I'm being watched, and rise slowly to my feet.

For a heartbeat, I stand to attention. Waiting.

One.

Two.

And then I see it.

Breathing becomes difficult at the appearance of two red eyes staring at me from between the trees.

Then four.

Then six.

Backing up towards the now anxious horse who kicks at the dirt under, I don't take my focus off the red orbs that appear all around me.

A soft vibrating growl rumbles through the trees.

The weapon in my hand seems like a toy, when, as one, seven mighty beasts step out of the darkness, teeth bared.

I think my heart actually stops at the sheer size of the wolf shaped, grotesque animals now growling at me. Their matted, black fur so thick and putrid that the next step I take is more to get away from the smell than fear.

Calculating my chances at survival, I realise there is no way I can win this battle. Deep in my soul I know I won't go down easily, I've come too far. I've endured too much already for this to be my end, and if it is, well then…I'll take some of these monsters with me.

Moving fast, I cut Toppin free from the tree he's attached to in the hopes that he'll be fast enough to outrun them. He rears back and sprints into the night. I spin back around in time to dive out of the way of the supernatural beast that lunges at me.

Rolling, I sit up in time to smash the hilt of my sword against the next one's jaw. It's breath causing me to gag.

Two of them chase Toppin into the darkness while the remaining five back up and begin to circle me.

Years of training cannot prepare me for what happens next.

Jumping and diving, I'm able to plunge my sword into the thick belly of one of my attackers as razor sharp teeth cut through the flesh of my calf.

My scream fills the world.

Panting and fighting back the sheer terror of dying, I grab at one of the burning logs from the fire.

Hands burning, I throw the blazing weapon at the next beast running at me. It's yelp is a muffled sound in my ears and before I can celebrate the small victory, I'm smashed in the side.

Hitting the ground hard enough to rattle my teeth, a beast lands on top me and all I can do turn my face and wait for the killing blow.

CHAPTER TWENTY TWO

A mighty roar shakes my bones and before I can register what's happening, the weight and smell of the animal is ripped off me. Curled against the ground, I keep my head covered when the forest erupts in sounds of battle. It's loud and vicious and terrifying.

Dazed and a little confused, I finally get my wits about me and sit up while trying to make sense of what I'm seeing. I know instantly who the man is who kicks and laughs while killing two of the animals at once with his long sword.

I'm reminded of the exquisite way Ever-Green moved on the road when I first met him and find myself lost in the beauty of his battle dance once again. Every muscle in his body tenses as he kills. One beast at a time. His war cry drowns out all other noises.

It doesn't take him long to dispose of another wolf-monster before they all run off into the night.

The man throws his head back and laughs a sound so joyful. He's acting like fighting against monsters is the best fun a person can have, then stretches out his arms in a sort of victory pose. I watch in perplexed wonder at how excited he is and actually shuffle backwards a little when he swings around and stares down at me as if remembering that I'm here.

If I thought Ever-Green was gorgeous before, I was wrong. With his face lit up in excitement and joy like this, he is.... *breathtaking*. There's a weird need in my soul to push up against his warmth and trace the lines of his face with my tongue. It's intense, strange, and a little unlike me.

Yes, I notice men. I've had a small number of lovers. Not many and nothing that went beyond a night or two. With an upbringing and lineage like mine, you don't really find pleasure in relationships like that. They fill a need and that's about it.

I don't have the luxury of falling in love like an average person. I have a duty and a King for a father, meaning my fate was always to marry a lord like Hamish Highben.

Reminding myself of my betrothal is not something I want to consider right now. I'm sure it'll be terrible and miserable, and frankly, I probably won't live to see past this damn road, so I guess it's not something I should be worried about anyways.

The oversized male bends down before me and studies me with such intensity that I don't move a muscle. Like prey caught in the gaze of a predator, I sit without moving.

He smells like something wild. Raw. Masculine. Spicy. With his body so close to mine, I feel like I'm seeing him for the first time. His soft brown, shoulder-length hair begs to be touched. His sculptured features appear fake, as if one of the King's favourite artists has hand crafted his face. I never knew a man could look so good, and I live my life around 'beautiful' people.

Shaking his head with a small smile, he states, 'now, I'm winning. That puts me in top position of who should be thanked.'

Of all the things he could say....Jaw hitting the cold, hard ground, I have to pick it up before I bite back with, 'you're an ass.'

All beauty, but a complete arrogant dickhead.

He turns his attention to my calf and grunts. 'I know,' he says while shrugging his broad shoulders like he doesn't care what I think of him. He pokes my calf and I fight the urge to slap his hand out of the way.

'This needs to be cleaned. I have some salve in my bag and a campfire not too far from here. Lucky I was close, the *wolven* are a formidable opponent.'

As the fight leaves my system, all that remains is pain and confusion. My body hurts. My head is pounding. *What just happened? How did he get here? What is a Wolven?*

'What're you talking about? What's a *wolven*? And why do you keep popping up. Are you stalking me?' My voice gets higher and higher as I lose control over my emotions. I got attacked by monsters that smelt like faeces. My mind is all fuzzy and the shaking in my body is starting to make my teeth clap together.

Ever-Green stays quiet and I watch, hyper focused, on those green depths as they soften slightly. His expression isn't the one I'm used to and it freaks me out even more. I've built a persona of him in my head. He's an arsehole, he's not kind. If he's kind then he must think I'm going to die from my wound or something equally as terrifying. The faeces monster probably has all kinds of questionable dirt under his nails, which is all now in my leg.

'Wolven are ancient beasts that prowl and hunt in these woods,' Ever-Green explains calmly.

I feel the tension in my shoulders slip a little at the energy surrounding him. He doesn't appear to be saying my last rights or running around trying to find his *salve* or whatever he said he has at his camp. Or he could know I'm a lost cause and is thinking to keep me around to rob me once I die.

'Okay,' I whisper, my lip wobbling a little, which he definitely sees, and I definitely hate myself for. 'You didn't answer my other question.' I sniffle and avert my gaze so that he can't see my little mini meltdown. I have to stay strong or I won't survive this quest.

'Which question? May I?' he asks, studying my injured calf.

I nod just before he lifts my leg into his hands to get a better look at the throbbing wound. I observe the way his face hardens a little as he mumbles under his breath about how silly I am to have stayed out here in the open.

'So, are you following me?' My voice quivers. His hands are unbelievably warm.

I don't think he's going to reply but he does eventually in that same, calming tone. 'I made camp just over the other set of trees. I had no idea you were here until a horse came running and interrupted my peace. Seems we might be heading in the same direction.'

Attention snagging over the information about my horse, I sit straighter. 'Toppin! Is he okay?'

'Your horse is fine. I told him to stay in my camp. Can you walk? This needs to be cleaned.'

Not able to stand on my own, I take Ever-Green's hand, which he promptly drops just before he briskly walks away.

'Come,' he demands over his shoulder. His voice is gobbled up by the heavy darkness as he disappears into the trees and I wonder if I misunderstood him when he said that he *told* my horse to stay in his camp.

I must have hit my head because I follow the strange man who has been showing up randomly on this journey.

CHAPTER TWENTY THREE

I don't know if it's the injury or the fact that I haven't spoken to someone properly in weeks, or that he saved my life, but when Green-Eyes asks me my name, I blurt it out. My calf is on fire and whatever Ever-Green is doing while cleaning my wound is hurting more than the attack. Trying to collect the words and shove them back in my mouth, I end up stuttering and muttering and pretending like I'm joking. Ever-Green just laughs like I'm simple and sits at ease in the forest like he didn't just take on a pack of...whatever those things were—wolven? There is a concern that they could still be out there.

'Susyri? As in the King's illegitimate daughter?'

'Yes.' No point denying it now, it's been said and there is nothing I can do.

'So, those bastards at the tavern who were going to use you for that reward *actually* had it right. You're the princess with the bounty on her head.'

That damn laughter is infuriating and I think he sees the way I flinch at the word he just used to describe the men who attacked me.

I hate that word *bastard*. I've heard it way too much in my life. It's always said as either a fact or an insult. Sometimes both, and always to remind me of what I am in this world.

Shaking his head with a final chuckle, Ever-Green just keeps on working on my leg.

'Don't laugh at me. And who are you?'

I don't think he's going to answer me at first. Finally he speaks, and again, I'm lost in his deeply masculine voice. 'You can call me Zeke. And I'm laughing because it's not often that I'm surprised, and you telling me who you are is very surprising. You should go home, Princess. You're better off in your cosy castle. You have no business being out here.'

Wincing at the pain of his touch, I try to pull my leg from his grasp, the movement futile against his hold. 'Sorry,' he says softly and he truly seems to mean it.

I know he isn't trying to hurt me, don't ask me how, but I do. It's like how I know that he's no real threat to my safety. Our interactions have proven that, or maybe I'm just too trusting, like when I was in the town where I was assaulted and nearly murdered for money.

'I don't live in the castle. I live in a small apartment at the back of the estate.' I hate the pain in my voice and the way I try to instinctively pull away once more from his touch.

His only reply is a questioning glance before returning to cleaning the bite on my calf. The fire of the wound slowly disappears as he wipes away the dirt and grime.

When I asked what was in the bowl he filled with a salve from his bag, he just said mostly water and herbs. It doesn't smell like the ointment you might be given by the castle healers. The stench of that shit makes you question if you'd rather take your chance with your injury. This smells minty and fresh.

'I'm illegitimate. I'm lucky to be breathing considering how much the Queen despises me. Stupid cow and her whiny voice is probably loving that I'm gone. I can just imagine the joy she's having telling everyone that I left in fear. Abandoning the King in his last days.'

'She sounds like a great woman.'

I chuckle despite myself and smile slowly when he looks me in the eye. Zeke watches me closely for a moment before going back to my injuries. 'Thank you for saving me.'

His hands stop working for a moment before they go back to what he's doing.

'Why are you helping me though? You could've left me, it's the game we've been playing since the first time we met.'

I comply when he tells me to hold the cloths he's using. 'It's not every day that a small girl would stop on a road to help a stranger who is outnumbered.'

Shrugging off his statement, I keep my focus on my leg. I don't know if it's just the firelight but it looks almost healed already. 'It's what anyone would do.'

'No, Princess, it isn't.' Zeke gets up and walks to the fire. 'Why are you out here on your own? Shouldn't you be with the King? Your father is gravely ill, is he not?'

Nodding, I sigh. 'Yeah, he is. That's why I'm here on this damn quest.'

That has his attention lift back to me. 'Quest?'

I watch his brows knot with his question, like that word intrigues him or something.

I'm not sure why I draw out the necklace from under my tunic. Holding it in my hand, I study how the firelight plays along the jewel. It seems so much brighter tonight. The colour is magnificent.

Zeke spins dramatically like something touched his back and he looks me dead in the eye before his gaze moves slowly down to the necklace in my hand. For a moment, I feel the need to grip it tight and run away. However, I watch the emotions that cross his face before it returns to the unbothered expression it normally holds.

I'm left feeling like I may have imagined what I saw.

Swallowing my trepidation, I conclude that it must be the drama of tonight that made me see things. I tuck the necklace safely back under my tunic.

We fall into an awkward, tense silence, and I swear I hear him cuss under his breath.

'Who gave that to you?' Zeke eventually asks, his entire demeanour has changed. He comes back over to me with a clean bowl of medicinal water. Kneeling down, he grabs my left hand, inspects the burns on them and then taking back the cloth, he begins to clean my palm. His touch sends small sparks of shivers down my spine.

Again, I'm not sure what has me decide to tell him the story.

'I met a woman. She said that I have to follow the Tilman Road until I reach the Dead Forest.

That I needed to find the gift returned, whatever that means, and get past the monster that guards the road out. She said once I do that, then I'll be granted an audience with the Alpha Lord of the Ekalus. I have to tell him my story, show him the emerald and ask for his blood. That it would save my father.'

Zeke's eyes rise slowly from my hand to my face. One eyebrow cocked he says, 'his blood? You think the Alpha Lord of the Ekalus is going to just cut his hand for some human princess and give you his blood? Whatever you think you'll find at Ekalus Peak is a fantasy. The Ekalus do not care if your father lives or dies.' He snickers, the sound screams that I'm a fool.

Bristling, I snap, 'I know how it sounds.'

'Do you?' he questions like I might be daft. He's working on my right palm now. 'Because that story sounds crazy and I can't believe that you'd head off on some quest, all on your own, with an emerald stone around your neck, looking for the Dead Forest so that you can meet the Ekalus Alpha Lord.'

'I know—'

'No,' he cuts me off and rises with the bowl.

Looking down at my hands, I can't believe how good they feel.

'You have no idea what you're doing, Susyri.'

Trying to work out if he is reprimanding me or not, I end up saying, 'I need to try and save my father, Zeke. Nothing else matters. Not just because if he dies, I will too, but because it's my duty as his daughter to find a cure. It is my duty to this kingdom to save him.'

Zeke has his back to me but I see his shoulders tense before he shakes his head. 'Fuck!' he swears and then he walks away.

Chapter Twenty Four

'You know, no one forced you to come with me.'

Laughing like what I've just said was the best joke he's ever heard, Zeke smiles. That infuriating, mesmerising laughter has been grating on my nerves all morning. I have no idea why I agreed to have him come along and if I truly think about it, I don't actually think he asked. Nor do I think I actually tried to stop him.

I'm lost as to how this happened really. It might be because I needed his help getting on my horse this morning and that my leg is beyond sore despite how good it looked when I woke.

'Why are you coming anyway?' I question again, looking over my shoulder for the hundredth time to see him still there on his white stallion, following along happily like we are going on a lovely adventure.

I'm still sceptical about how he acquired such a magnificent beast. I reckon he stole it, even though he told me it was a gift. The poor thing doesn't even have a name. *What kind of brute doesn't name his horse?*

I pat Toppin and whisper to him sweet nothings about how I'd never not name him.

'I told you, I have nothing better to do. And I can't just let you head on your quest after the trouble you seem to land yourself in constantly *and* you're injured. What kind of citizen of this kingdom would I be if I let our princess take on the Tilman Road, on her own?' *Why does he sound like he is mocking me?* 'And besides, I've never been in the Dead Forest and it sounds fun.'

'Are you drunk?' I've suspected he's been drinking since I woke up to him staring intensely into the fire like he was hypnotised.

'Maybe a little.' He grins and it's the most gorgeous grin I've ever seen. I roll my eyes and contemplate if I really need a drunk fool on this quest with me. I've seen him fight with that long sword he has strapped to the side of his white stallion. He is good and I could use an extra set of eyes and ears, especially after I was attacked. Twice.

Focusing back on the road ahead, I try and fail to not let his words get to me. 'Is this how the rest of this trip is going to be? You saying stupid shit and me having to listen to it?'

He ignores me.

Anxiety begins to bloom in my chest at the thought of the rest of this quest. It seems like nothing is going right and having Zeke here is making me all confused. I secretly would love some company. I feel a great deal more comfortable with him beside me, despite the arsehole himself, but I have to do this alone. That's what the woman said.

'What's with the face?'

Frowning, I try to understand what he means. 'What face?'

'That look. You don't want me to come with you.'

His response takes me off guard. 'No. I don't know. I just...that woman, the one who gave me this—' I press my hand against the emerald tucked safely away, mostly just to check that it's still there, '—she said I have to do this alone. That this was my quest. I know it sounds insane. I have this fear that she'd know if I didn't, like she might come from the trees and tell me I failed.'

I sound like I need serious help, from a healer. However, it's the truth. I'm so obsessed with doing everything right for my father and for all of this to not be some sick joke that I feel I have to do everything right.

I've never thought myself superstitious, guess I was wrong.

'What did she say exactly?'

Too lost in my own head, it takes me a moment to understand who Zeke means. 'She said I have to do this alone.' I swear, I just said that.

'Tell me her exact words, Princess,' Zeke grumbles, clearly unimpressed with my tone.

Hating the way he calls me that, I work through my memory of that night. The darkness. The way she just appeared out of nowhere. Her hair...I remember being envious of her hair. She was stunning.

Sighing, I recount what she said. Her words are ingrained in my mind, and will be for the rest of my life. My dreams have been of that woman and her voice, and that hair. 'She said that I have to travel to Ekalus Peak. Along the Tilman Road and then through the Dead Forest. I have to find the gift returned, get past the monster guarding the exit and take no other way. She said that I have to start this quest alone and that this was my journey to take.'

I'm screwed.

While it's not very strong of me, the idea of having Zeke around is starting to sound nice. I wouldn't have to be afraid all the time. From the moment I left the castle, I think I've been living in a state of fight or flight. Everything that has happened so far on this trip hasn't helped.

'You said you have to start the trip alone. She didn't say end the trip alone.'

Again, his voice draws me from my thoughts and I honestly have no idea what he's talking about. 'What?'

'You just said that you had to start the journey alone.'

'No, she...' Shutting my mouth, I contemplate what he's just pointed out.

Did she?

Running the words over and over in my head, my jaw falls open at the realisation that he's right. She did say that I had to *start* the quest alone. She said nothing about ending it alone.

'Do you think?' Fresh hope sparks in my chest and I sit straighter and look to Zeke for reassurance.

I don't know what he sees on my face but after staring for a little too long, he nods slowly. 'Yes, Susyri. Words have meaning, Princess. Phrasing has meaning, and when you're discussing a *Messenger*, it is all there is.'

Totally lost, I eat my bottom lip and try to decipher his words. It's impossible. 'What did you call her?'

'The woman you met in the garden. She was a *Messenger*.'

Tsking loudly, I can't help but roll my eyes. 'She was not.'

Messengers are creatures of tales. They're said to be otherworldly beings, neither allied to humans or Ekalus. If you believe the lore, they're commanded by a higher power, a power stronger than the winged predators. Stories about how they interfere in human affairs are always requested at feasts. I've heard tales of wars having started with a visit from a Messenger. Or of peace declared from information given by those otherworldly creatures. My favourite is the kingdom of Dwyman, which fell a thousand years ago, all as a result of the meddling of Messengers. That story is full of intrigue and politics and is the greatest cautionary tale of court politics.

Personally, I believe that humans like to blame outside forces for their shortcomings. I don't believe that *Messengers* actually exist outside of stories.

During my lessons as a child, I'd get so frustrated because none of my elderly tutors could tell me if they were evil or neutral or even if they were good. Every story has multiple points of view. Each one blaming the *Messengers* or painting them as peacemakers. It was confusing. At least with the Ekalus, we know they're predators. Beings that have no mercy.

'Why would a *Messenger* come to me?' I scoff, dismissing his idea wholeheartedly. Nonsense.

'Messengers only interfere when the world is hanging on two paths. Or when lovers need a nudge in the right direction.' My next eye roll is completely involuntary. 'Maybe you're destined for great things, Susyri.'

'Huh!' I can't contain my laughter. He can't be serious. I'm a bastard. A no one. I'm a product of desire and sin.

Throwing me a sidelong look, Zeke nods his head as if he knows something I don't and I shut my mouth and repress the need to give him a very unlady-like gesture.

CHAPTER TWENTY FIVE

We stop and only because of our horses. It's unkind to push them anymore today and I groan when I slip out of the saddle and land on sore leg. We travelled all day and I'm feeling the wound badly now.

Finding a small, cleared area just off the road in the thin forest, Zeke goes about setting up a small campfire while I watch awkwardly. The sun is low in the sky and deep shades of reds and oranges illuminate the world. I was so confident with my decision to stay with Zeke but now that I'll be spending my first full night with a strange man, on my own, I'm starting to feel a little uneasy.

Zeke doesn't say anything about my behaviour or how I'm hovering near Toppin. He just claps his hands when the fire begins to burn brightly. Rising, he declares that he's going to go and get us some food and disappears into the trees.

He didn't take his sword or any weapons that I can see. I have no idea what kind of food he's expecting to find in the forest.

I think he must be the oddest person I've ever met in my life, and I live at court. There are some very weird nobles in that place.

Yet, here I am, staying with him and telling him my secrets. For all I know, he could sell me out in the next town for the reward.

I'm a fool.

I should leave, but the fire is burning and I'm cold and lonely. So, I pull out my bedroll and some food from the bag attached to Toppin. I make myself busy setting up a small sleeping spot on the other side of the fire from where Zeke laid his own bedroll out.

I feel good about the distance between us. Toppin is close to my back and the fire is at my front. It's a good position, not that I'll be able to sleep.

Coming to attention, I grab the hilt of the dagger at my belt and jump up when I hear a noise from the growing darkness. I relax when Zeke appears from between the trees.

With a big, joyous grin on his face, the big guy declares, 'I caught dinner!' in his booming, loud voice while holding up four fish like they're some kind of prize.

He seems mighty impressed with himself and I bite my lip to keep from giggling at the way his chest seems to puff out at his own importance. Swaggering to the fire, he begins to use sticks and pieces of wood to create a little stove which he gets to work using to cook our meal.

He does all of this whilst I sit, watching in trepidation and awe of how efficient he is. I feel like a complete failure. Like I have been naively trying to survive on this road and thinking I was doing a good enough job.

What an idiot I am.

I don't know how to make a big fire like this or how to hunt or catch fish. Zeke wasn't even gone for that long. Definitely not long enough to catch four freakin' fish, gut them and bring them back to cook.

Eating in silence, I did bring out a few bits and pieces from my own bag to contribute to the meal. Some bread and a spice from the castle that Zeke sniffed before adding to his fish like I might poison him. He ate some, so obviously it passed the test. He sniffs everything, I've noticed. It's weird.

The sun has gone down and I shiver at the bitterness of the wind that sweeps through the trees, reminding me of how exposed we are out here. I swear if I look long enough at the trees, I see red eyes and big teeth. I reckon those damn *wolven* are going to haunt my dreams.

Clearing my throat, I try to fill the space with noise and ask, 'so, do you have family?' *I sound like an idiot.* Shaking my head at my own stupidity, I go back to pushing the pieces of fish around the small travel plate Zeke served my portion on.

I don't think he's going to answer me until he says, 'Yep.'

Glaring over the fire at his evasive reply, I drop the subject. He clearly doesn't want to talk. I eat half my fish before he states, 'you know, I still don't understand why you're doing this, Princess.'

I can't help but sigh and try to figure out what to say. 'I told you, to save my father. And I told you, I don't have a title, so stop calling me princess.'

The firelight plays along Zeke's face as I stare at him from across it. His green eyes don't leave my face and I swallow the well of nervousness that fills my body at the intensity of his gaze. I feel exposed. In danger. There is something about him. Something I can't put my finger on.

'Your father doesn't treat you well from what you told me on the road today.'

I regretted that instantly. Zeke asked me what my father was like and I told him I didn't really know. He found that very interesting.

'Why save him? And don't give me all that honour shit. I don't believe it. I believe you don't want to die and that you think you will if the Queen gains power, but there must be more. The likelihood of you surviving this quest is very slim.'

'Thanks for the confidence,' I mumble and take a moment to think through my reply.

'Well, it was slim until I showed up,' he declares and I can see his head expanding with his ego. The smug ass throws me a very arrogant, very male look. I emphasise my next eye roll to make sure that he can see it.

Laughing, Zeke mumbles a few words that make no sense, something about the universe and their games.

'I don't believe that you're on this quest just because of the love you have for your father.'

Love. That word has me shuffle where I sit and Zeke seems to watch me like a hawk, like he knows how uncomfortable I am.

My father doesn't love me.

I haven't felt loved since my mother was alive and that was a long time ago now. So, I just give the same response I gave him earlier in the day.

'I've grown up learning of the kingdom. I've been trained in politics and defence. Our kingdom needs the King. Without him, it'd be chaos.'

'So, you do it for your kingdom?' Gods, he is infuriating.

'I guess. I do love my father despite everything. And he has taken care of me. I'm his daughter. It's my duty to find the Alpha Lord and ask for his help. I don't know what else to say to you, Zeke. Everything I've said today is true. I'm here for selfish reasons as well. I don't want to die. *And* I'm doing this for the kingdom. There's nothing else for me to say.'

Zeke doesn't reply, he seems deep in thought and I leave my empty plate beside my bedroll to clean later. With a full belly and the exhaustion of the day, I lay down with the intent of just resting my eyes.

'You're not like anyone I've ever met.'

Stopping from trying to get semi-comfortable on the hard forest floor, I look over at the male staring into the flames.

'I'm just a daughter doing her duty,' I reply quietly.

I hear him huff the word 'duty' before I turn my back and close my eyes.

CHAPTER TWENTY SIX

I wake with a start from a dream filled with emerald eyes and jewels that shine the same colour. I gasp loudly, staring up at the male stand over me. I find myself locked in his gaze, unable to move. Dream and reality get all muddled in my head.

The cold wind of morning has every hair on my body stand on end and I shiver. On instinct, my hand goes to touch the top of my tunic.

I don't feel the jewel.

Quickly looking down to find it has slipped from out of my shirt, I find myself unsure what to do.

Gaze flying back to Zeke, I don't move under his intense scrutiny. He isn't looking directly at me anymore, his focus is on the emerald that hangs from my neck, on full display.

Zeke eyes the stone and I can't decipher the expression on his face. Pained, maybe. Annoyed, definitely.

For a moment I fear that he's going to try and take it. A part of me believes he want to destroy it. His energy is volatile and I swear I see him shudder slightly. His skin appears to ripple.

Eventually, he just shakes his head and grunts at me to hurry along.

'You were sleeping like the dead. We should start moving.'

I watch as he strides away, knowing that something is wrong.

We've been on the road for a few hours and Zeke reckons we should keep pushing until nightfall. I reckon I should leave him and find somewhere to rest, my leg is hurting me today.

We haven't seen eye-to-eye since I woke to him hovering over me. When I was 'too slow' at getting ready to travel, he demanded that I hurry up.

Grumpy prick.

'Here, eat this.'

Spinning in the saddle, I catch the red ball that flies at my head before it hits me in the face.

'You didn't eat the food I made this morning to break our fast.'

'You mean the questionable meat you made over the fire with some kind of weird herb you took out of your bag that made it turn black?' I say to the apple in my hand. Well, I think it's an apple. It looks fake. The colour is spectacular and beyond anything I've ever seen.

'Don't comment until you try it. That herb makes any *questionable* meat taste like eating in the grand dome of the Ekalus.'

'Been to the grand dome of the Ekalus recently have you?' I grumble, having no idea what a grand-dome even means.

My brow furrows at the pensive expression on his face. He is too busy digging around in his bag to notice me staring.

'Not recently,' he teases and throws me a wink that has me both scowl and hold my breath at the sheer beauty. 'Now, eat.' He was very concerned with me eating this morning and huffed and puffed around the camp when I said I wasn't hungry.

To keep the peace, I turn the fruit in my hand to make sure it's actually an apple before I bite into it.

Flavour explodes on my tongue and I experience a fundamental moment in life. I question every piece of fruit I've eaten.

I've never tasted anything so exquisite before.

'Holy shit.' My mouth is full of apple but I don't care. I munch away, loving every bite.

'Holy shit indeed.' Zeke chuckles.

'Where did you get these?'

I hear crunching and look back to see Zeke enjoying his own apple. 'Found it at the market.'

There's a part of me that doesn't believe him and another part that doesn't care, because I'm having a moment with my apple.

Finishing it off, I throw it into the trees and wipe my hands on my pants. I really wanted to lick the juices off but think better of it.

I contemplate asking him for another one.

Zeke kicks his horse up to my side. Leaning over, he holds out another, offering it to me.

A story I read once in my studies comes to mind. Gaze locked in those intense eyes, I can't help but remember it. An apple offered in temptation and a human who fell into the trap of sin.

He grins again and I swallow the nerves that creep up the back of my throat. It's as if he knows what I'm thinking.

Reaching over, I take the offering and then shiver when the most intense feeling shoots through my core as our fingers brush together.

Zeke sits back in his seat, smug and whistling as he kicks his horse further up the road. I'm left to wonder what has just happened and fearing that I haven't fully thought through this situation.

We travel for half the day in a comfortable routine.

I've informed Zeke numerous times that if he wants to go his own way, I wouldn't have any hard feelings. He just says that he's heading down the Tilman Road anyway and sticking together isn't a big deal.

Every meal, he hunts and I have been getting better at making a fire, under his tutelage.

He continues to question what I'm doing and there are moments when I catch him looking sadly at the flames when he thinks I'm asleep. There is a pain surrounding the man that makes me question my opinion of him. I can tell that he has a great deal on his mind. I find I enjoy his company, even when he's barking orders at me.

He is actually really sweet and always waits for me to start eating before he does and helps me when I struggle with my sore leg.

I never thought I'd think this but it's nice having him around.

CHAPTER TWENTY SEVEN

'Stop.'

I do instantly. The tension in Zeke's shoulders and the way he's looking around has me grip the handle of my sword. I search the trees. The Road. The sky.

'What is it?' I whisper.

I see no danger.

Zeke jumps from his horse and pulls it up beside mine. He grabs the reins of both our animals and with a few glances my way, the man grumbles and digs around in his saddlebag before bringing out a thick, black, tattered looking cloak.

'Here,' he says, throwing the garment at me like he's angry. 'Put this on. And cover your hair.'

'My hair?' Confused, I fumble with the cloak and eventually wrap it around myself.

'Yes, the damn colour is like a beacon to your beauty, and right now, I need you to be as quiet and as unattractive as possible.'

Unattractive? Did he just... *why am I blushing?*

Hiding my face, I go to ask him what he means and shut my mouth with a clank when I hear what has him so rattled. Horses. Lots of horses.

'What—'

'Just stay quiet. Keep your eyes down and don't say anything,' Zeke cuts me off and before I can tell him to shove his male arsehole-ness up his arse, I see the group of riders coming towards us.

Their navy uniform makes my throat close up.

This is the first time I've seen the uniform of the King's army on this road and after my run-in with the thugs hoping to kill me for the bounty on my head, I quickly cover my entire body with the coat, my hair included.

Even though no solider out here would know who I am, my heart still beats erratically in my chest.

Wrapping myself in the intoxicating scent that clings to the cloak, it helps me to calm my nerves as the group approaches.

I see ten, maybe twelve horsemen.

I can't see if there are any more towards the back of the group. I know enough about the army and it's structure through Master Kieran that it wouldn't surprise me if there were four more in the trees, scouting.

They're all in the navy uniform I look at each day living in the barracks, all with my father's crest on their breast.

Releasing a breath I didn't realise I was holding, I wasn't aware how worried I was that my father may have passed while I was out here being attacked by monsters. At least now I know my father is alive. If he wasn't, they wouldn't be wearing it.

The man at the front, the one with the C stitched in gold amongst the crest, catches my attention instantly. He's very handsome, with shoulder length mousey blonde hair and blue eyes.

Before I know it, he and I are staring.

The Captain assesses me and I quickly avert my gaze, cursing myself for not playing the part Zeke told me to. I blame my upbringing. I was never taught to keep quiet and not make eye contact.

'Sir, you're a long way from town, where are you headed?' the Captain asks, his voice firm, yet curious. I can still feel his gaze.

'My wife and I are travelling to the town of Creator and from there we go to her parents in Sistiema.' A lie. Zeke and I decided that staying out of towns was the best decision, we are heading straight to the Dead Forest.

'Farmers are you? Creator is full of farmers.' I can hear the scepticism in the Captain's tone. The arrogance.

Three soldiers move their horses around us. It takes everything I have to keep my eyes downcast.

'My wife's family are farmers. I work with horses.' I have no idea what Zeke is doing and chance a glance down at him.

Zeke is like a different person.

Gone is the carefree energy that normally surrounds him and his typical arrogant swagger as he bows his head slightly.

His face loses the light that I've become accustomed to and I question how old he is. Originally, I thought he was maybe a few years older than my twenty four, but now I think I may be wrong. He stands with such confidence, like he knows he's the biggest threat out here on the road. Like nothing these men can do or say will affect him. It's obvious that these soldiers are getting frustrated by their lack of power to intimidate him, which is clearly something they are unaccustomed to.

It makes me smile into the cloak. He holds himself like a noble which contradicts everything I've seen so far.

I don't have time to ponder the puzzle that is Zeke for long because the soldier to my left brings his horse right up to my side, making Toppin stomp in warning.

Zeke pulls my horse closer and rests his large hand on his head, calming Toppin instantly. I'm surprisingly jealous of my horse and silently reprimand that silly, girly thought.

'That would explain these exquisite beasts. You own these horses?' There's an undercurrent of accusation from the soldier who questions Zeke. Heart quickening, I know this is going to turn bad.

'Yes,' my 'husband' replies easily.

'Your names, Sir,' the Captain questions in a friendly tone that oddly sounds like a threat.

'Mr Colt, Captain. My name is Zeke Colt. My wife's name is Betty.'

It takes everything in me to not react to the name, his lies fall so smoothly from his lips that I question a few things that have happened since I've met him. *Is his name actually Zeke?*

'And you, Captain, what is your name?'

I don't think the man is going to answer but he does with a smile, 'Captain Laurence Jorge. Now, you both wouldn't mind if we checked your belongings.' It's not a question. Captain Jorge says something to the soldiers that I miss because I'm too busy staring at my husband to see what he's going to do.

'And if I said that I did?' Zeke enquires.

Holding my breath, I'm no longer pretending to be the submissive wife and lift my gaze to watch the Captain's reaction. He smirks at me and it causes the hair on my arms to stand on end. He gives me the creeps.

'We can do this the easy way or the hard way, Mr Colt. And with your wife here, I suggest you choose the easy way. We wouldn't want her to get hurt.'

CHAPTER TWENTY EIGHT

The three closest soldiers jump off their horses to come over and start checking our belongings.

I nod when my 'husband' steps to my side and offers to help me get down from Toppin. He clearly doesn't want me anywhere near the strange men. I don't miss the way he quickly slips his hand into my saddlebag and pockets my 'illegal' map into his jacket.

I do my best to move the coat I'm wearing so that I help cover what he's doing from the soldiers moving around us and lean into his outstretched arms.

Zeke lifts me like I weigh nothing, his gaze screaming for me to keep my cool and places me down gently behind him. I wince when I put pressure on my bad leg and nod when he quietly checks to see if I'm all right.

'Are you unwell, madam?'

Attention snapping to the Captain watching us closely, I shake my head and silently thank Zeke when he lets him know that I hurt myself yesterday.

'Would you like our healer to look at it?' the man asks, indicating to the long line of soldiers behind him.

'No, thank you,' I answer, ignoring the warning glare Zeke throws me.

I don't fight the way Zeke pulls me into his side, tucking me securely against his body. 'Why are they doing this?' I whisper up at my fake husband when we eventually lose the interest of the Captain for a moment. I think he is very focused on the things being pulled out of my bag, like my undergarments.

Sleaze.

There is a powerlessness in this situation that I've never felt before.

Watching people who perceive themselves as having more power than me use it in such a way is confronting and unsettling.

I hate that I just have to stand here and take their abuse of power in fear of what they will do if I speak up. Being attacked at the tavern was an experience I never, ever, want to happen again but this, this is something else.

'Just stay quiet. They'll leave us alone soon.'

Zeke keeps me close. His strong, muscular arms are heavy around my shoulders.

I fight with the need to draw in his exquisite scent.

We stand awkwardly, watching our bags being invaded. It's violating.

The inside of my cheek hurts as I bite on it to keep my mouth shut. When the soldier looking through my bag grabs one of the material pieces I use to cover my breasts, I'm stopped from telling him to fuck off when Zeke grips my hand and squeezes it in warning.

My clothes get thrown all over the road.

They aren't being so flippant with Zeke's belongings. They aren't really looking at his stuff, just mine.

'We'll be on our way soon,' Captain Jorge reassures us, completely unfazed by the injustice of what's happening.

One of my daggers is the next to be thrown on the ground and I fear for a moment that they might recognise the intricate pattern on the hilt. It's not a cheap weapon and was made by one of the best bladesmiths in the kingdom, something they should question.

They don't notice, which says a great deal about them.

A pair of my undergarments is pulled from the bag and lifted into the air by one man and Zeke has to yank me to his side the moment I open my mouth. I reluctantly snap it shut and suck in a breath at the pain that shoots up my leg.

'I doubt whatever you are looking for is within my wife's undergarments.' It's hard not to hear the warning in my companions tone and isn't missed by the soldier with his filthy hands on my stuff.

'Maybe if you tell me what it is you expect to find, I can help.'

The Captain smiles and I no longer find him attractive. He's creeping me out.

I make a mental note of this incident so that if I do survive this quest and get back to Master Kieran, I can complain.

I know my advisor would love to know how men declaring themselves King Soldiers behave out here in our kingdom. He'd be appalled. He'd have them stripped of their crests.

'We're looking for a woman. A run-away from the castle, the King's bastard actually. Seems like she has gone missing. The Queen is concerned for her safety.'

Holy shit! I feel the colour drain from my face. The Captain is looking too hard at me and I turn my head to hide the expression on my face.

'Have you seen anyone travelling on their own?'

'No.' Zeke doesn't miss a beat. Actually, his calmness is scary. 'It's just my wife and I. We haven't seen anyone in a few days.'

There's a heartbeat of silence while I stare at Zeke's side, afraid to draw any attention to myself. These men might work under my father's crest but there's a bounty on my head, dead or alive, and I don't trust anyone on this damn road.

'Hmmm,' the Captain replies and it makes my blood run cold. He doesn't believe us, I just know it.

Zeke is still holding my hand and squeezes it gently as if reassuring me that he has everything under control.

'I also don't think they're going to find a lost princess in my wife's underwear,' Zeke fires back and receives a deep chuckle from the man watching us closely from atop his horse.

'That's enough,' the Captain declares and his little lackey's move away and mount their horses.

Atop his own stallion like he is the King himself, Captain Jorge bows his head at us. 'Enjoy your journey, Mr Colt. I suspect we'll meet on this road again.'

We watch them all leave and I can't help but feel like Captain Jorge might be right.

CHAPTER TWENTY NINE

I'm furious, like I haven't stop ranting and raving, kind of furious. I've complained about everything, from having to pick my clothes up off the dirty road, to how much trouble those men are going to be in when I get back to the castle, to how miserable this entire trip is. It's dramatic and a little vicious and when Zeke eventually tells me to give it a rest, I'm kinda surprised he didn't shut me up sooner.

'I'm angry!' I growl, gripping Toppin's reins so hard that my nails dig into my palms.

'I hadn't noticed,' Zeke replies like a smartass. He's not really focused on me, he's looking around like he can see something I can't. I'm too frustrated to care what the next problem is and almost jump out of my seat when the first rumble of thunder shakes the ground below us.

'Great!' I half shout. 'That's all I need, more rain. Why is everything against me! I'm just trying to save my father!' My rage is boiling over and I'm finding it really hard to contain it right now.

'Not just rain, Princess. I think we're in for a massive storm.'

Head snapping over to the male riding beside me, I frown at the worry in his tone and look up to see the darkening sky with unease.

'We need to get to the next town.'

'It's still a fair distance away,' I state, trepidation lacing each word. I can already feel the fear of the impending chaos creeping over my skin.

Ever-green eyes collide with mine and I listen without hesitation when Zeke tells me to ride, and ride fast.

We get into town just as the rain becomes torrential and when Zeke opens the doors to the monstrous tavern in the centre of the town square, he practically pushes me inside.

The place is alive with activity. The heat from a gigantic fireplace has me nearly fall to the floor in a weeping mess, praying to the heavens. I'm drenched and starving. The smell of roasted meats and vegetables has me listen without complaining when Zeke points to a table in the back corner and tells me he'll get us some food and enquire about a room.

The Road Tavern is packed full of travellers trying to get out of the rain. Groups sit together, talking loudly. There are three minstrels playing music on the other side of the space. Hooded individuals sit hunched over their food. Women. Men. The place is alive, and while I hate the crowd, I can't help but feel the buzz in the air made by the amount of chatter and laughter.

Pulling the hood off my head, I remove my travel bag and Zeke's coat and hang them both on the back of the chair. They're dripping with water and I feel a lot better now that I'm no longer outside.

Trying to relax, I spy a couple of groups of men sitting close to my table openly staring. Avoiding their gaze, I watch the activity around me with interest. This is probably the biggest tavern I've been in since starting this quest.

Uneasy, I remember what Zeke said on the road about my hair and am just about to grab the coat again when two mugs of ale are dropped on the rectangular table before me.

'That was a bit of a fight,' Zeke proclaims, completely unaware of the anxiety I was feeling. He slumps down in the chair across from me and the poor wood groans under his weight.

Throwing a quick glance at the tables surrounding us, I notice that all the men have stopped leering. A wave of emotion floods my system and I blink over at the man who takes a mighty swig of his ale. I guess having him around is good on many levels.

Wiping his mouth with the back of his sleeve, in the most un-gentlemanly way, Zeke continues telling me what happened at the counter, like I asked him to elaborate. 'The owner's going to let me know if he has rooms for us. He thinks there's a group leaving but isn't sure with the rain.'

Frowning, I play with the engravements on the wooden mug and consider what our options would be if we can't find somewhere.

'We'll work something out,' Zeke states, like I voiced my worries out loud.

CHAPTER THIRTY

Sitting across from Zeke, I feel the most comfortable I've felt this entire trip. Actually, maybe even ever. Like in my entire life.

Right now, I'm not a bastard princess. I don't have to play the game of court politics. I can't let my hair down like this in the castle grounds.

Drinking and laughing, I even end up in a lively conversation with a group of travellers on the table beside ours. They don't talk with caution to not offend me or have to choose their words. They don't fake to be friendly, they just are.

When they leave, I try to give Zeke my attention again, he doesn't say much and just grunts when I try to ask him questions about his life.

So I focus on the music and dancing happening on the other side of the tavern. The beat of the current song is lively and I tap my foot along to the jingle while drinking my ale.

The food is taking forever to get to the table, which is understandable with the mass of people inside this place. More just keep filing in through the large double doors too.

The music changes when a bard steps in the middle of the room. A hush falls over the crowd as he announces himself with the hype and grandeur of someone of his craft. The energy in the tavern makes me all giddy as I sit at the end of my seat, eager to listen.

Everyone claps and hoots at the man as he begins his tale of love and woe. It's funny in parts and sad in others and I sit in silent rapture as his words paint a picture in my mind.

Some say the young village woman was walking in the meadow,
Some say she was at the river where the current flows,
But this bard knows it was nothing as grand.
Working in her garden, she simply dug up the jewel, the colour of blood and dirty sand.
Perplexed, she sat, and examined the piece, that burnt hot in her palm, yet soothed.
For days, she waited at her table alone, she felt the tide of impending doom.
It called to something, she knew in her bones, and her heart pounded just out of beat. Until one day he came, with wings of red, and declared her the source of his heat.

Snickering and jeering followed the bards words and I giggled into my mug at the inappropriate comments happening around the place.

Shocked, the young woman rejected the claim and yet the beast of firewings didn't move.
He waited and watched and tended her fields, his devotion he wanted to prove.

No word or demand would deter him, oh no.
You see, unbeknownst to her, the girl found a heartstone.
A rare treasure that won her his heart.

I think I'm the only one in this entire tavern who hasn't heard this song because I'm the only one to gasp.

Transfixed, I listen, loving this story more than I can imagine.

The legend explains, it would have hurt her with pain unless she was his true soul-mate.
She cried and she begged and eventually took him to bed.
The predator with eyes of deep red.

The tavern erupts in cheers at the inuendo and the gesture that the bard makes.

He stops for dramatic effect and I laugh quietly at the comments made around the place.

Zeke just sits, unfazed, staring at the bard like this is the most boring story he's ever heard.

I roll my eyes involuntarily.

I know what you're thinking, I'm gonna find me a stone
But ladies, I'm sorry to say.
That one does not come by a stone everyday
And if you did find one, the Ekalus will take you away.

Up to his mountain, the young girl was taken, never to be seen from again.
A shifter. A beast. A predator. A man.
And a heartstone of blood and dirty sand.

I clap with the rest of the tavern.

The bard bows and waves and holds his hand over his chest and relents eventually when everyone asks for more. The music turns then and a ballad is sung of adventure and dragons and ghouls.

Feeling eyes on me, I turn to see Zeke staring and while I can't read the expression on his face, I don't let him ruin my fun because that is what I'm having. Drinking and clapping along, I'm invited to a drinking game by the hairy men on the table beside ours when they catch me watching. The rules are a little confusing about taking a drink every time the bard says a word, so I just take a big swig of ale every time they do and cheer along with them.

I don't remember the last time I've laughed so hard.

CHAPTER THIRTY ONE

'Zeke! Son of a bitch, I thought that was you!'

A large man with a long, thick beard and a round face appears at the table.

'Henry, it's been a long time.'

My jaw nearly hits the table at the tone of Zeke's voice and I quickly look over at him to see that he is...smiling, and it seems genuine.

I didn't even know that he could smile like that.

'It has been, my friend!' Henry's booming voice fills the tavern and I find myself instantly liking him. He has kind brown eyes and seems pretty bulky under his dark travel clothes. 'Last time I saw you, you were fighting a tavern full of men over a card game, naked.'

Grinning wide at the piece of information, Zeke throws me a glare that screams to not ask. 'Naked?' I question, not listening and not surprised in the least.

'Don't,' Zeke warns and I chuckle, mostly because I think I might have had too much ale and mostly because I'm now forming images in my mind of Zeke fighting, naked. I shiver. It must be the ale.

'And who is this spectacular being?' Henry asks with a flourish of movement as he bows deeply. 'Lady, I am Henry Groom. Merchant of rare and exotic treasures. Lover of pretty woman, and a good friend to your companion.'

'And a complete pain in the arse,' Zeke adds much to Henry's mock horror.

More people appear behind Henry's shoulder. Two more muscular men and a woman with her hair tied tightly at the base of her neck.

They're all middle-aged and full of energy.

The woman is the only one who greets Zeke. He doesn't seem too happy to see her and gives a tight nod in her general direction. My interest peaks. The pair start a tight-lipped conversation about something to do with the last time Zeke saw her, which the woman doesn't seem happy about either. I think he might owe her money or something. I'm dying to know more. Every time I open my mouth and look at Zeke for answers, he just shuts me down with a hard look. It makes me grin wider and wider until I laugh after the fourth glare.

The sound seems to make Henry happy and he quickly introduces me to Burk, a big guy with dirty blonde-grey streaked hair and a beard that touches his chest. Galligan, a stocky man with unkept orange hair, large arms and an axe strapped to his belt. Fi, the woman with the clear dislike of Zeke nods her head, she seems more interested in fighting with Galligan about how much food to order. The man just nods and waves off her last comment and walks toward the bar. I guess that Fi and Burk are related by the hair and similar features. She's looks like she could command an army.

I like her instantly and she takes the seat beside mine with one last scoff towards Zeke. The others pull some more chairs over.

Henry positions himself at the end of the table between Zeke and I. 'So, you're not going to introduce us, Zeke my man?' Henry is staring as if waiting for me to tell him everything about myself.

'Oh um...' I don't think I've ever felt so tongued tied. After what happened on the road, I quickly glance over at Zeke for some guidance on what to say and then something behind his shoulder catches my attention. Fear creeps up my spine. I swear the music and chatter dies down when everyone realises who has just walked in from the storm. The group of uniformed soldiers take in the patrons with an air of arrogance and superiority. Spotting Captain Jorge, I duck my head. The action not missed by the people around me. Zeke picks up on the energy change in the tavern instantly and is already looking over his shoulder.

Even Henry and his crew stiffen. 'Friends of ours?'

'They gave us a hard time on the road,' Zeke explains, he doesn't seem bothered and promptly ignores the newcomers.

I, on the other hand, am trying to hide my face and contemplate if grabbing Zeke's cloak would draw attention to myself.

'Hmmm, they've been giving everyone a hard time looking for this *Princess*,' Fi gripes.

'I heard they've been up and down this road for the last week. They're arresting groups of people they thought looked suspicious.'

My stomach drops into my butt.

'Stopped us just outside of Lochnee,' Burk adds and I can't help but feel there is more to the story.

CHAPTER THIRTY TWO

'Did you all see who just came in?' Galligan states the moment he's back with a tray full of ale mugs.

He drops them on the table like a pro and starts handing them out. I get one plonked down in front of me, my small thanks is drowned out by the noise in the tavern. The appearance of the soldiers has worn off and they are now being ignored by the majority of the men and women enjoying their night.

Not me. I can't help but watch Captain Jorge as he struts to the bar and then over to a long table on the other side of the inn where a group was promptly kicked off to make room for them. I hate the way they smile like they have all the authority in the kingdom.

It infuriates me. These men use my father's name, my family name, to get what they want. It makes me so mad. I'd give anything to be able to stand right now and tell them who I am and what I'll do with this information. Instead, I sit back in my chair, watching behind the rim of my mug in secret. Silently fuming and raging at my life.

I'm so lost in thought that I miss everything that's said around the table.

I can't seem to care about what the group is discussing.

All I care about is getting the hell out of the tavern so that I can continue on my doomed quest. I shouldn't be in here laughing and drinking. I should be out there, completing this mission before my father dies. Before I die!

It's on that thought of death that the colour drains from my face when Captain Jorge turns his head from his companions to stare directly at me.

My gasp is loud and I quickly avert my gaze.

My heart pounds erratically within my chest and I shake my head when Zeke grumbles a, 'what's wrong', from across the table.

'Nothing,' I reply quickly when he probs again, this time in that *true-arrogant-prick style*. I know that he doesn't believe me because he keeps side-eyeing me as I slink down in my chair and try not to overreact.

Not that it does much to help. Within the next heartbeat, the table goes completely silent, maybe even the entire tavern does. I have no idea because an incessant ringing starts in my ears as my blood begins to pound painfully through my veins.

'Good evening Mr Colt and Mrs Colt,' Captain Jorge's gaze slowly drifts from my 'husband', around the table, to land pointedly on me.

I practically hear Henry's jaw hit the top of the table. The woman beside me mumbles, 'no fucking way,' under her breath. It just adds to the way my stomach churns.

Captain Jorge needs to believe that I'm married to Zeke and he's starting to notice the shocked expressions on the faces of the others around us. I don't know if it's the fact that the blood has rushed out of my face and into my feet or a play of the light in the room, but I swear he smirks, like he just found treasure.

'Captain Jorge, how lucky we are to be running into you again.' Glaring at the man across from me, I try to kick him under the table and think I end up kicking the big, hairy guy next to him because Burk lowers his mug of ale and side-eyes the woman next to me. Fi doesn't seem to notice, thank the heavens.

'The storm has brought many people into town tonight,' the Captain replies smoothly.

'How fortunate for us all,' Zeke states, his voice carrying around the tavern and that's when I notice that there are a number of patrons watching the exchange.

I wonder if Captain Jorge understands that he isn't welcome. He probably does. I can tell by the way his shoulders sit, all high and mighty, and by the arrogant set to his jaw.

'Would you join us, Captain?'

I bite the inside of my mouth to keep from demanding my *husband* explain what it is he's doing. Captain Jorge grins but it's more of a scowl than a smile. He's probably annoyed that his presence isn't intimidating Zeke or the others at the table who are ignoring him.

Not me.

No, I'm fidgeting with my hair and have contemplated six times if I should grab the coat hanging on the chair to cover it.

Blaming Zeke and what he said on the road, I'm just a ball of pent-up energy so that when the innkeeper and a server appears on the other side of the table and begins to place our food before us, I jump and squeak a little sound.

I become the centre of attention. If I could read minds, I know that Zeke would be reprimanding me soundly and telling me to calm down. He's glaring at me like I stole his coin purse.

'Are you well, Mrs Colt?'

Gods, why does Captain Jorge sound so amused. I want to smack him and then smack myself.

'She is,' Zeke answers smoothly. 'Afraid of the storm,' he adds, frowning at me over the brim of his mug, which he brings to his lips.

I stay quiet and nod solemnly and wish that I was better at pretending. I was never very good at playing pretend when I was a child. I blame my mother. She always said that games were for children who didn't have important lessons to learn.

The innkeeper doesn't seem to care about any of us or the Captain as he says, 'Mr Colt, I managed to get the two rooms, side-by-side, for you and your companion, like you requested. You can pay the tab in the morning before you leave.'

Why! Why did I have to take a sip just as the innkeeper spoke! I choke and splutter my ale when I register what he's just said.

'Two rooms?' Captain Jorge enquires, still with that infuriating smirk on his face. 'You need two rooms for you and your wife, Mr Colt?'

This is it. I've been discovered. He's going to arrest us and torture me, and I'll cave. I'm not very good with pain. Then he'll take me back to the castle where the Queen will kill me—publicly.

Fi begins to pat my back while I cough up the liquid that went down the wrong way.

Zeke, the expert liar that he is, appears to be confused by the entire situation and smoothly exclaims that he didn't ask for two rooms. 'I'm sorry, there must have been some mistake. We are only in need of one but thank you all the same.'

Now, I genuinely have no idea what is causing me to want to vomit more. Captain Jorge discovering that I'm the woman he is looking for or having to share the same room with Zeke.

'Whatever,' the keeper sighs, clearly unfazed and too busy for this conversation. He hobbles away.

There's a heartbeat of silence before Captain Jorge bows his head at me slightly and wishes us a lovely evening. 'I'm sure we will see you very soon.'

Gods, the way he looks directly at me has me swallow the bile that rises in the back of my throat. I realise that I'm playing with my hair again and drop my hands dramatically.

I have no idea how I've survived this long.

I watch Captain Jorge walk away with a swagger of a man that knows he has power.

Again, everything is too silent around the table until Henry shrieks, 'you're married!'

CHAPTER THIRTY THREE

'I still can't believe it,' Henry exclaims for the hundredth time. He does this thing where he chuckles to himself, shakes his head and drinks from his mug. 'Married. Zeke. Just can't believe it.'

'Oh for the love of the Gods, Henry get over it! It's not like Zeke is getting any younger, he was bound to get married one of these days.'

Hoping that Fi can see my appreciation in the small 'thank you' I throw her, I try and stomach at least some of the food in front of me.

The pie is hot.

The meat could either be rabbit or venison, or something else entirely. I really don't want to know.

Ignoring the little voice in my head that keeps telling me that it isn't one of the safe meats, I shovel it in my mouth, not so much tasting as just needing to fill my stomach.

'I know that. It's just...it's Zeke, the grumpy fuck. And look at Betty!'

Herny's voice is getting higher and he's now pointing at me like whatever he is saying can be concluded by getting everyone to look at me.

The two hairy men down the table huff a small sound that I think may be a sound of amusement and Fi stares before she nods. 'He's right, Zeke. It makes no sense.'

Zeke scowls dramatically.

'I don't get it,' I confess with a mouth full of pastry which has Zeke throw that scowl my way. 'What?' I have no idea how me saying that got me a glare.

Fi pats my knee sympathetically and Henry studies me so intensely that I have to avert my gaze. 'You really don't, do you Betty?' He whistles and I'm so confused that I just continue to eat. 'Where did you find this treasure, Zeke?'

'Damn meddling fate,' he mumbles into his own food but I could be wrong.

'Well, tell us how you met, Betty. I'd love to hear the story.' I thought I liked this man when we first met but now I'm finding his wide grin and questions really irritating.

'Um,' I stammer, trying to catch Zeke's eye. He doesn't seem to care about what we're talking about. He's gulping down his ale and people watching.

Fine. 'I saved his life.' That has him paying attention.

Henry claps and cheers like that's the best thing that he has ever heard. Zeke grunts like he thinks I'm delusional.

'I did!' I emphasise.

'You think you did, but I had everything under control.' The arrogant prick takes a big swig of his ale like he's the king of this tavern.

Snorting a very unladylike sound, I shrug. 'Think whatever you want.' Those Ever-Green eyes lift to catch me in their intense gaze. I get lost in the colour.

The emerald is a humming heat between my breasts. The feeling magnifies the way my heart flutters in my chest. Zeke is the most stunning person I have ever seen. That jawline. The hair. The cheekbones and those lips. He's an arsehole and he laughs at me all the time but sitting here in this noisy tavern with my belly full, I realise that I'd like nothing more than to feel those lips on mine.

The ale has definitely reached my head.

'Was it on the farm?'

I un-stick my gaze from Zeke's and frown over at Henry. 'What?'

'Did you save him at the farm?'

I think my brain got all fried for a moment because I have no idea what he's saying.

'Where you live. Where you and Zeke met?'

What?

'Yes,' Zeke answers, eyeballing me again. 'It was at the farm, with one of the horses.'

Oh shit. We are supposed to be farmers and horse traders. Far out, I was about to ruin everything.

Quickly grabbing my drink to have something to do with my shaking hands, I try to focus on something else in the room and find Captain Jorge staring again.

CHAPTER THIRTY FOUR

Zeke appears as happy as I do walking down the dark narrow corridor on the third floor of the tavern, heading to room six. Now that we've left the noisy, warm hall downstairs, I become more aware of the sound of the rain hitting the roof of the tavern. I'm praying for there to be no rain tomorrow when Zeke stops abruptly and starts fiddling with the key.

Standing close to his back, I wrap myself in his coat and watch as three drunk men come from the stairs and head loudly to their rooms.

I couldn't eat after I noticed that Captain Jorge was watching and when Zeke asked earlier if I was all right, I could barely nod my head. I don't know what made him tell the group that we were done for the night and asked if I wanted to head up to bed.

Henry made all sorts of lude comments when we left. My *husband* didn't seem to care as much as I did. Since hearing Henry wish us a great night, my heart hasn't stopped pounding erratically in my chest.

Every time Zeke brushed his hand on my arm, my lower back, or between my shoulder blades to guide me through the tavern, up the stairs and to the room, it's becoming harder and harder to breathe.

I've never shared a room with a man before. It's not appropriate for me to be seen with company like that in my apartment. If my father found out, I'd be in deep, deep trouble. He never cared what I did or who's company I kept, as long as I was discreet and quiet.

'Maybe we should just head down and ask the innkeeper for the other roo...' I slap my mouth closed at the appearance of the group at the entrance of the corridor.

Zeke stops jiggling the key in the lock, eyes me and then straightens when he realises what has me shut up.

'Captain Jorge.' My husband dips his head respectfully and I easily mould into his side when he places a large hand on my hip and pulls me close.

'The *Colts*, what a coincidence that I'll be staying right next door to you,' Captain Jorge exclaims with that creepy smile on his face. He pulls out his key and opens the neighbouring door easily.

Zeke pushes ours open with one hand. It squeaks loudly. 'Yes, a coincidence,' is all he says as he pushes me inside our room.

'Please wait a while before enjoying your wife, Sir. Or none of us will be getting any sleep with the noise I'm sure you two can make.'

I stiffen and the pressure on my back increases as I'm pushed harder into the room. I don't catch what Zeke says in return, the sound of blood pumping in my ears makes it hard to hear.

He slams the door shut after us, blocking out the sound of male laughter now coming from the corridor.

'That man is a predator.' I feel gross and anxious and angry.

I'm really, really angry.

It's the only emotion I feel as I stare in hatred at the small bed taking up the entire space. It's the smallest quarters I've ever seen in my life and I truly believe in that moment that the heavens hate me.

In three steps, I hit the side of the bed, the one facing the door. The other side is pushed against the wall.

'That's offensive to predators,' Zeke absently states and drops our bags on the scuffed wooden floors. Then he makes a weird, funny sounding noise that has me pull my focus from the disastrous bed situation. He has obviously just noticed where we will be sleeping tonight.

I don't know if it's the really bad lighting in this place or because I'm exhausted, but I swear his eyes darken. Like to almost fully black.

Doing a double take, I know I'm just seeing things because he's still the attractive, ever-green-eyed, arrogant man who I have to share a bed with tonight.

I'd rather be out in the storm.

At least...I tell myself that.

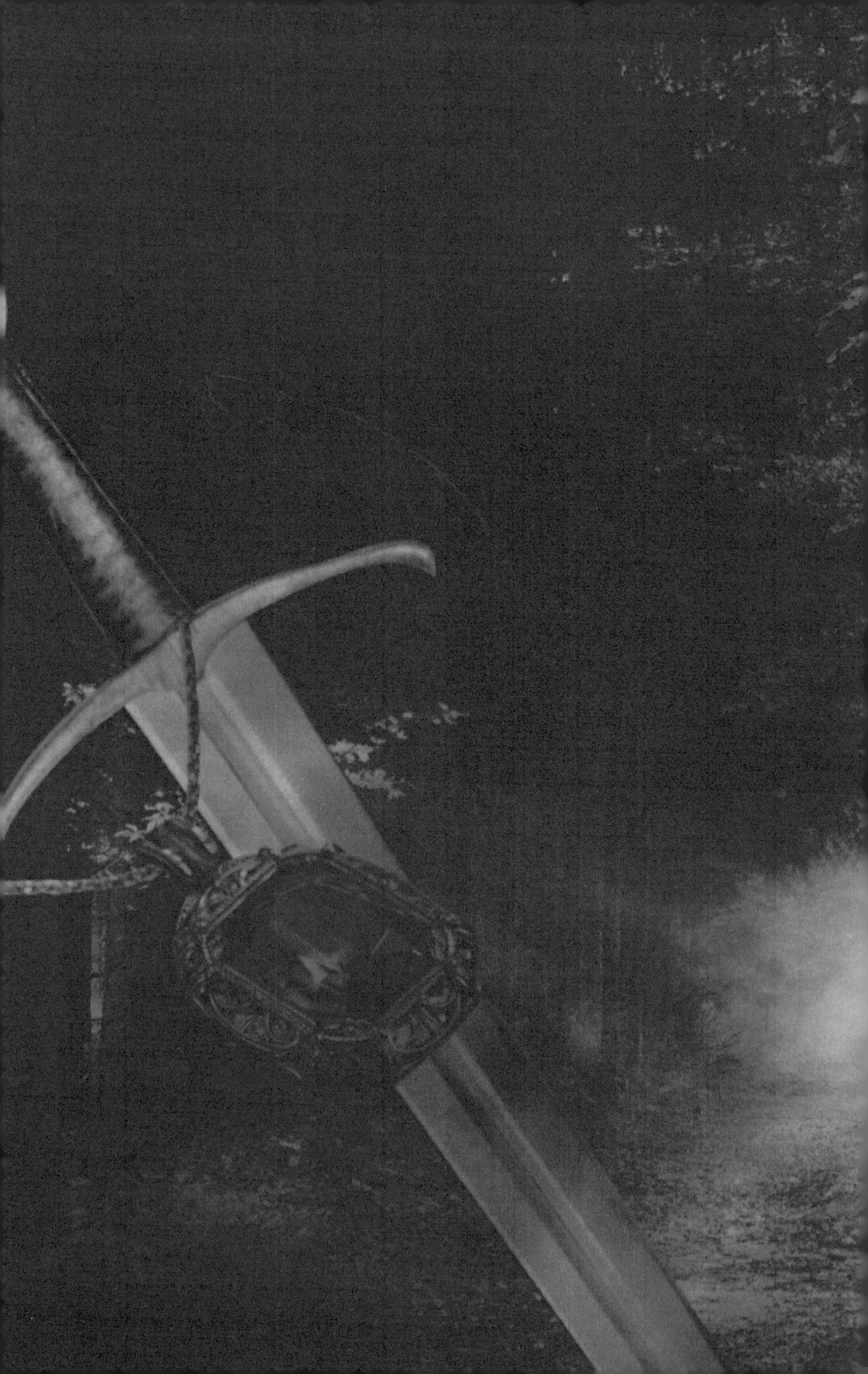

CHAPTER THIRTY FIVE

I get myself in and out of the bathing room as quickly as I can.

Not even the fact that I haven't had the luxury of running water for forever could've kept me in that disgusting room. Granted it's not much better when I step into the small, dark space with the tiny, compact bed.

Slamming the door behind me with my sandaled foot, because there was no way I was going barefoot on those disgusting tiles, I shiver. 'Blah, that was gross.'

'That's why I refused to go in there.'

I can't help the way my lip pulls back in annoyance. 'I thought it was because you're a slob and would rather smell like an animal.' I'm lying. He doesn't smell like an animal, quite the opposite. Actually the entire, tiny cell-like bedroom smells like him. Like sunshine and rain on grass and something else...something sinful.

Zeke grunts. He looks very comfortable with his head on his arms, eyes closed and relaxing. I have noticed that his shirt is changed, so I guess that's a plus.

I've also noticed that the blanket has pooled around his waist and I can see the bare skin between the end of his shirt and the top of his pants. The overwhelming need to tell him to pull his it down is hard to ignore. The fact that it affects me is making me mad.

Mad at myself, *and him.*

I try to take my time stuffing my old clothes into my bag. I've changed into more travel clothes in case I need to run in the middle of the night. I learnt that after the last tavern debacle.

Remembering that messed-up night, I double check the locks on the door are all in place. It takes all my effort to push down my anxiety over the flimsy clip that someone thinks is good enough to keep intruders out of this room. Frankly, it's probably a waste of time even having it.

'Princess, the doors are locked. It's late. We should leave here early tomorrow. Just go to sleep.'

Right. Sleep.

Turning around slowly, I stand like an awkward fool just observing Zeke wondering what I should do. He takes up most of the bed.

He cracks one eye open. They travel down my face to the necklace I didn't realise I was playing with. I drop the emerald jewel and it thuds against my chest. His expression is hard to decipher.

'What are you doing?'

'I...I'm...' I really don't know what I'm doing, or what to say. 'I've never, you know...' I try really hard to shut my mouth, but the words are falling out of it too fast.

I swear his brow rises up to his hairline. 'You've never slept before?'

'No.' Huffing, I cross my arms. Such a smartass. 'I've just never slept with someone in a bed before.'

'Ever?' he asks, clearly not understanding why this is a problem.

'Why is that so hard to believe?'

Shrugging, he sits up a little, now looking at me with an expression I've never seen before. 'It's not.'

'Then why are you looking at me like that?' I demand, really self-consciously.

'I'm not looking at you like anything.'

He is. It's a total condescending kind of look as if he thinks I'm being a child or something. I swear he rolls his eyes and lies back down.

'Just get into the bed, Susyri. It's late. I won't touch you, I promise.' Gods, he doesn't have to sound like touching me would be the most disgusting thing he could ever do.

Scoffing, I mumble, 'you don't have to say it like that,' but he's already closed his eyes and has gone back to ignoring me. 'That's not what I'm worried about.' I take a small step toward the bed and stop. I'm playing with the emerald again.

'Oh my Gods, what now?' Zeke demands, he's still got his eyes closed.

'I can't get into the bed. There isn't room. You might have to move over,' I say, probably a little forcibly. There is no way that I'm climbing over him to lie between him and the wall.

This time when he cracks his green eyes open, they are full of annoyance. 'Princess, there is no way that I'm moving over.'

For heaven's sake, he is so difficult and I go to tell him that but he continues, 'I'll be between the bed and the door and you will be right there.' He points to the small sliver of space beside him.

'Why does being near the door matter? Now who's being a child!'

Again, he gives me that 'don't be daft' expression. 'Because if someone knocks through that door brandishing a long sword and tries to chop off your head, they'd have to get through me first.'

My heart beats so painfully slow as every single word he just said seeps into my brain. Did he...is he saying... 'Oh...'

'Yeah, ohhh,' he mimics, and honestly, I don't know how to feel right now. I want to melt into the stone floor or maybe fan my now heated face or open the door and run as fast as I can. The struggle is real.

'Okay,' I whisper and with great difficulty I manage to hop-crawl-jump over him with minimal touching.

It takes me a while to get comfy because there really isn't any space and when I pull the blankets up to my chin, I finally take a breath.

Kicking some of the blankets around, as I hate being so tucked in, I jump out of my skin when Zeke shrieks, 'holy fucking heavens!'

I squeal a, 'what?' searching for some kind of dangerous insect or knife-wielding warrior or an Ekalus looking at us from the tiny window on the other wall.

'You're feet are freezing!'

Staring wide eyed at the ridiculous male beside me, I giggle, then chuckle, and then laugh myself to tears.

'It's not funny! Seriously woman, what is wrong with your feet? Put some damn socks on or something!' He seems really mad and I seriously can't stop laughing.

Not able to help it, I reach over and touch my toes to his leg and he actually squeals.

'Stop!'

My stomach hurts, I'm laughing so hard. 'Sorry, I couldn't help myself. My feet are always cold.'

'You have some serious issues then. Honestly, you should see a healer.' Zeke mumbles a string of profanities as he sits up and starts tucking my feet into the layers of blankets we're using.

Seemingly satisfied when I'm unable to move them at all, he lies back down with a heavy sigh.

Eating my bottom lip, I thank him and get a solid grunt in return.

'Go to sleep.'

'Yes, *husband*.' I don't know why I say it. Maybe it's so that he looks at me one last time before we go to sleep. I win, because he does.

'You're a menace, *wife*.' Gods, my heart skips a damn beat. He is so close. So warm. So…masculine. He frowns slightly at whatever he sees on my face and tells me once more to sleep.

Yawning, I nod and quickly turn to face the wall. 'Good night, Zeke.'

'Good night, Princess.'

With his body pressed against my back and the wall to my front, I drift off.

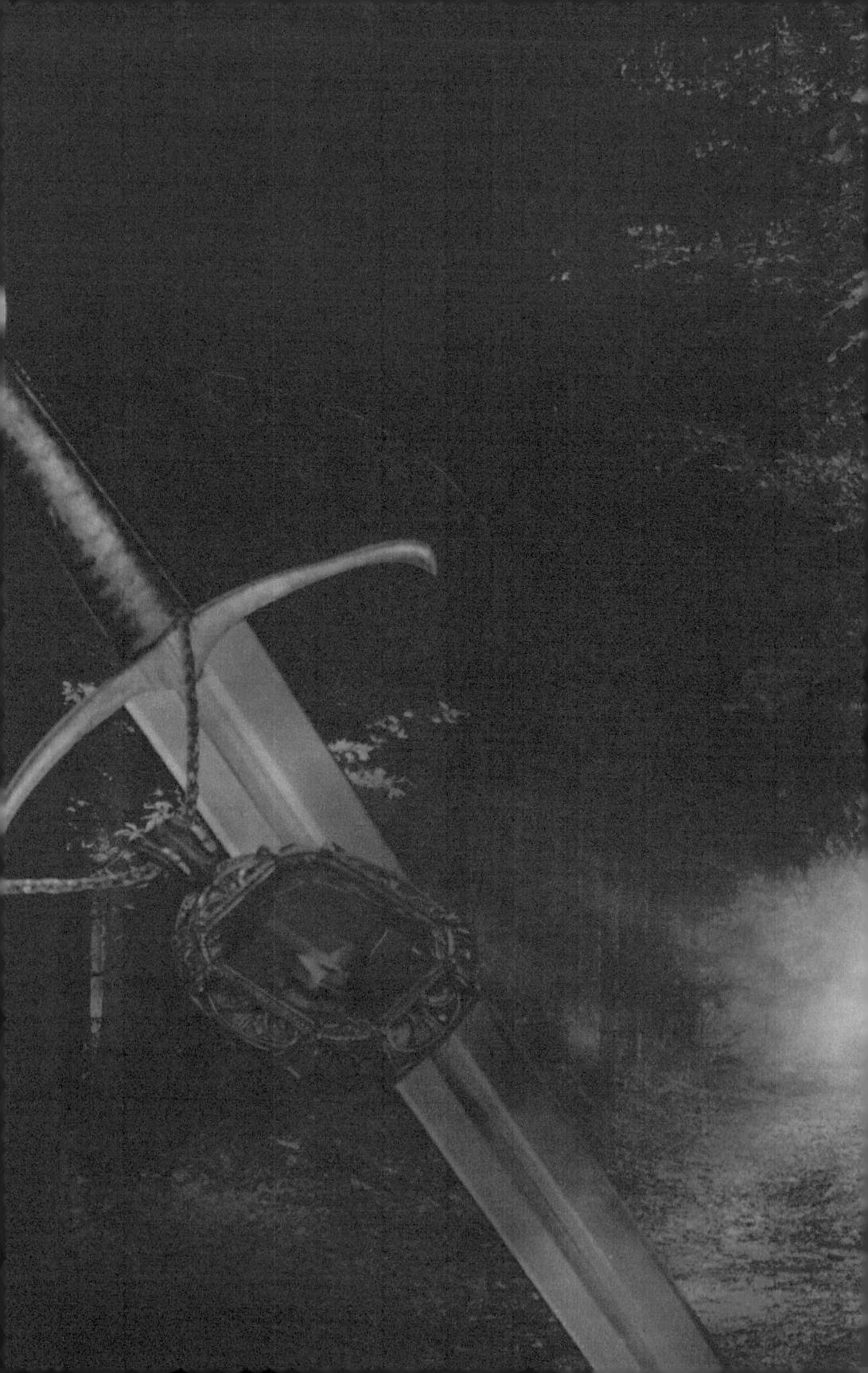

CHAPTER THIRTY SIX

I wake with a start, my mind on high alert.

A large hand across my chest keeps me from jumping up and I blink down at it and then over at the wide-awake man beside me to protest that he get his arm off my breasts.

The words die on my lips.

Zeke's focus is on the roof and he's looking at it like he's ready to jump out of bed and stab someone.

'What is it?' I whisper. His head is still against his pillow and that kinda makes me feel a little better. If there was a problem, he'd be out of bed...right?

'Shhh.' Gods he's infuriating.

I still, ears straining to understand what has every hair on my body stand on end. Zeke's body is touching mine and I swear the energy surrounding me has me all jittery and ready to run.

'I don't hear anything,' I whisper, quieter than I did last time, which still wins me a glare.

I'm about to open my mouth and say something else when I hear it. A soft sound. Barely audible, if I'm being honest. Like tiny little feet on the roof. Tap. Tap. Tap.

'What is—' My mouth shuts and I stare wide eyed at the male beside me when we hear a shout in the distance. And then another. And another. They sound closer or maybe they're louder.

My heart is in my throat and it's making it hard to breathe.

Gripping the arm that has me locked against the bed, I jump when a scream sounds from outside the door.

Chaos erupts in the hall.

Boots bang against the floor as if people are run up and down. Things crash. Glass breaks. The walls shake.

Men and women cry a bloodcurdling sound that has me whimper. It's horrible.

'Zeke, what's happening?' I squeak, unsure what to do. It's like I can't control my eyes. I'm frantically searching the roof, the windows, the door, waiting for death to come and get me. 'Is it the Ekalus or the wolven again?'

'Susyri!' My name is a command that cuts me off from my growing hysteria.

It is a demand for me to look at him, and I do.

Zeke's green eyes are intense.

'Breathe. In and Out.' I do and only because there's no ignoring his orders.

This Zeke is not the Zeke I've met before. There's no humour or the swag that he normally has.

I calm, only because he stares at me like this entire situation doesn't affect him at all. That no matter what issue we are about to face, he has everything under control.

I breathe.

'Good girl. Now, I need you to listen and follow every instruction that I give you. Can you do that?'

Nodding frantically, I agree instantly and jump when more shouting reaches our room. I need to run. I need to leave this tiny space. Something bad is happening, and staying here feels wrong.

An unnatural shriek outside has tears begin to rush down my cheeks. There is something out there.

'Zeke. What is that noise? What is happening?' The next sound is one of death. A slow, bloody death. Something thuds heavily against our door.

A large hand falls to the side of my face. The contact soothes my raging heart. 'It is the Xavar.'

'The...Xavar? The mythical pixies that eat people alive?' The room spins, I'm about to pass out. 'That doesn't...they don't exist—'

'They do!' he replies, truth dripping from every word. My entire world seems to shudder and shift. 'Susyri, you will be fine, I promise. Nothing is going to happen to you. Now, you're going to get up slowly and grab your bag. You'll do everything I say, when I say it.'

He waits and when I get a little more control over myself, I agree.

I nearly whimper when his hand slips from my face. I want him to put it back. I want to curl into his side and stay under the sheets and ignore the death and destruction happening in the corridor.

'Let's go.' Zeke hops off the bed and turns to offer me a hand, which I take without much thought. 'Grab your bag and put your shoes on.'

I do. The noises of death and mayhem haven't stopped. It's getting louder.

Zeke shoulders his saddle bag and we continually bump into each other as I clumsily slip on my boots. My hands are shaking violently so it takes a lot longer than it should.

Zeke notices. Gripping my upper arm, he helps me to slip on my shoes. When I fumble with the laces, he bends down before me and gently pushes my hands away.

When he gets up, he instructs me to turn around. Back to his front, I'm reminded of how much of a height difference there is between us.

'Now, I'm going to tie this over your eyes.'

A piece of cloth falls in front of my face and my stomach plummets into my feet. 'What? Why? No!'

'A Xaver hunts by locking their gaze on their prey. The moment you make eye contact, there's no escaping their sight. You can't look at a Xaver. They're faster than light. So small, that you won't be able to see death when he dives onto your face and eats your eyeballs first before devouring you slowly. You'll still be alive when they start eating you. They—'

'Okay, I get it!' I whisper-shout. I feel sick and take a deep breath before Zeke covers my eyes with the cloth, plunging the world into darkness.

'Hang on, what about you?' I ask, touching the cloth while he tightens it.

'Don't worry about me, Princess. The Xaver don't scare me.'

That's a weird thing to say but my brain can't process it right now.

'I need you to stay quiet, Susyri. Not a word. And don't take the blindfold off until I tell you.'

CHAPTER THIRTY SEVEN

In Zeke's arms, I hold on for dear life and try not to lose the contents of my stomach.

Zeke is carrying me. His arms are under my knees and wrapped around my back. I've got mine tightly around his neck, and on his instruction, I've buried my face into the crook between his shoulder and collar.

I feel that with my sight taken away, the sounds of terror and death have become heightened.

Zeke walks swiftly and calmly through the chaos.

At one point I hear him make a noise that shakes my entire body and all I can do is hold tighter.

I'm expecting him to complain that I'm choking him. He doesn't. Someone screams close to us and I bite the inside of my mouth to keep from making any noise. The noise of the Xaver are nothing I've ever heard in my life.

There aren't any words to explain the shriek-scream-squeak sound that seems to touch every nerve.

We're outside. His steps are softer. The noise isn't as intense and the chill of the night has me curl in harder to Zeke's body.

'Zeke! Zeke! Oh my heavens man, what is going on?' It's Henry. I totally forgot about Zeke's friends.

'You need to get out of here, Henry. Take the others and go,' Zeke snaps. He hasn't stopped walking and I really hope he's taking me to Toppin and Horse, the name I christened Zeke's beast a few days back.

'I can't find Burk,' Calligan announces to my left.

'What the fuck are those things?' Fi says somewhere to my right. 'And why is Betty blindfolded. Should we be blindfolded? Where is Burk!'

To my dismay, Zeke doesn't reply. He just keeps moving. I fight with myself to obey his order to stay quiet.

'Zeke,' Henry implores. I can hear them running behind us to keep up. 'I know you need to get Betty out of here. I know that you have an idea of what these things are. Please, we need you to help us find Burk and then we can help you both. I know something is going on for you two. Six of us together on whatever journey you are on is better than just two.'

'I doubt that,' Zeke replies, not faltering in his strides.

'Come on, Zeke. I just saw a man get his eyeballs eaten.'

The way Calligan says those words has me gag. Behind this darkness, my imagination is running wild right now.

'We can't leave my brother to die.'

Zeke stops abruptly and I feel a hand touch my back and slip away as if it was an accident. 'He is our friend, Zeke.' Henry sounds grief-stricken and lost.

Moving my arm from around Zeke's neck, I place my palm against his chest, my fingers brushing bare skin. 'Zeke,' I whisper so quietly that I don't know if he can hear me. 'Please, don't leave Burk to die. Henry is right. He is your friend. Don't choose me over another person.'

Zeke doesn't say a word and I can't see to understand what is happening.

He sighs, swears colourfully and then jumps into bossy arsehole mode. 'Fine! First, stop fucking looking around like that or it will be your eyeballs being eaten next.'

I can see in my mind how they would all react.

'Secondly, you need to get to the horses. Quickly. Move, now. Don't look at the Xaver. Keep your eyes on the ground and only look up when I say. Do you understand me? I'll get Betty to safety first and then come back to find Burk.' We move.

I know I should find it odd that they don't question what Zeke has said or that he is speaking of magical creatures of stories like he knows all of this with certainty. The group seem to trust him completely and I feel stupid for not asking how they all know each other at dinner.

'Get the horses. Get on them and leave. Now!'

There is a commotion to our left. Henry curses. Fi gasps and the sound of metal sliding out of their sheaths fills the air. That's when I hear the Xaver. The sound.

It will haunt me forever.

'Run!' Zeke commands. 'Do not look behind you. I'll find Burk but I can't guarantee he will be alive when I do. Henry, take Betty. Take her to my horse and get her on it. Don't look back. Ride hard.'

'No,' I whimper and try to pull the covers from my eyes. I'm stopped by a large hand that prohibits me from taking the blindfold off. 'Zeke!' I beseech.

'*Wife*, you will go with Henry. I will be right behind you.' I don't know how he gets me off him. I'm struggling with all my might. Zeke is so incredibly strong, and when I'm passed into another hard, male body, this time I don't curl into its warmth. I don't want Henry holding me. I have the overwhelming need to recoil.

'Are you sure? I can help.' Oh Gods, even Henry sounds worried.

'You are helping. Now, take her and go, Henry.'

The noise of Xaver has me cry out. 'No, Zeke. No. *I* can help.'

A heavy hand falls on my head. It's warm and my body leans towards it. 'You'll help me by doing as I say so I don't have to worry about you.' That shuts me up. 'Go with Henry. Leave the damn blindfold on and stay quiet. If you are attacked, stay *quiet*, Susi. Close your eyes and keep silent. They won't hurt you. I will find you, Princess. Now, go!'

I want to rage and fight and pull the cover from my eyes, however, I know that this isn't a situation I understand. While it's weird that Zeke seems to know so much about the Xaver, I trust him.

So why does leaving him behind feel like having my heart ripped out?

CHAPTER THIRTY EIGHT

I thought I was terrified before, I was wrong. When Zeke told Henry to go and we start moving again, I feel a fear like no other.

The realisation of leaving Zeke on his own to face those shrieking, tiny monsters that I thought were a myth, is like facing a horde of Xaver on my own.

Henry gets us to the horses safely and constantly tells me what he is doing before he does it. I'm up in a saddle with the voices of his crew around us. Fi seems to be praying for her brother's safety, over and over.

I hold on when Henry jumps up behind me and we fly through the night.

It's so disorientating riding with your eyes blindfolded. The horse I'm on is not Toppin and I just have to hope that he is here with us and that they didn't leave him behind.

Every hit of hooves on the hard ground reminds me of the growing distance between Zeke and I.

He stayed back. He could be dead. Eaten alive.

I taste blood, I'm biting my lip so hard to keep from making a noise. He told me to be quiet and so I'll be quiet.

'Not much further,' Henry promises and I wish I could tell him to keep it down. He's shouting over the wind in our ears. Shouting at his crew to keep up.

Zeke told us to be quiet.

We need to be quiet. They have to stop, yet to tell them to stop, I have to speak.

The stone beating against my chest begins to heat until it starts to burn my skin. It adds to my heightened state of fear. I have no idea if I can take any more.

Seriously, my heart is starting to flutter and skip beats. All I can hear is a phantom Xaver shrieking in the distance. I have to keep reminding myself that it's not real. That we are getting away from the madness of the tavern.

They can't travel as fast as horses, right?

It's disorientating. Being blindfolded doesn't help.

So, when I hear that haunting sound again, I don't take it seriously. Not until I hear the next shriek and the horse cries out and the man behind me swears loudly and colourfully.

My stomach falls into my butt.

'Xaver!' Henry shouts.

Fi cries out.

Calligan barks instructions.

Horse bucks.

Henry's grip slips.

He yells to me to hold on and then I'm ripping the blindfold off my head to understand what is happening.

Then I'm falling.

I hit the ground, hard. The pain is nothing like I've ever experienced.

By some miracle, I manage to keep my head and roll away from the horse stomping and screaming it's fear so that I don't get trampled.

It's dark. The only light is the moon which is throwing eerie shadows from the trees. The rocky road we were travelling on cuts into my skin.

'Run!' Henry shouts.

I comply. I can hear the Xaver. I can hear one of the men shouting in pain. Fi is bellowing a war cry that has me whimper.

I run as fast and as hard as I can into the trees.

Tears stream down my face.

Keeping my eyes fixed on the ground, I fall three times. I feel the impact on my shins and my hands, the skin ripping open, over and over.

Despite the pain, I don't stop. I push myself up and keep moving. The thought of death by little creatures eating me alive fuels my energy.

Noticing that everything is quiet now, I realise that I can no longer hear the battle on the road. Footsteps I thought I detected before are long gone and just as I begin to contemplate if I should slow down, I trip and fall straight on my face with an, 'ooomph.'

Air knocked out of me, I wheeze. Every breath sends a shock of agony through my entire body.

Seeing stars, I roll over with a groan and freeze. My heart jumps into my throat when I hear it.

Tap.

Tap.

Tap.

Tap.

The sound of tiny footsteps on the leaf, littered ground.

The sound of my doom.

CHAPTER THIRTY NINE

The cold hand of fear wraps around my neck, making it impossible to breathe as I lie as still as possible. My eyes hurt, I scrunch them shut so tightly. There's a deep-seated primal part of me that knows I'm surrounded by Xaver.

I can hear them clicking.

Terrified at the sound of their feet tapping on the forest floor, I try to remember to stay quiet.

I bite my lower lip, drawing blood, to keep from screaming out when tiny hands begin touching me all over. Never had I thought that this would be how I die. Eaten alive by tiny mythical creatures was not on my top ten list on the quest.

I thought I'd at least get to the Dead Forest. Maybe I was cocky enough to think I'd even get to Ekalus Peak. A small part of me believed I had a tiny chance at coming face-to-face with the Alpha Lord before I was murdered. I never thought I'd die here. On the Tilman Road. On my back. Frightened and alone. Barely half-way through my quest.

The clicking noises they're making has my skin crawl. There's a pressure on my chest and then tiny hands touch my face. Touch my closed eyelids and my bloody mouth.

I want to scream and cry and pray to the heavens for help, but I'm frozen in fear. I could try and run, though I'm not naive enough to think that it would save me.

I'm not ready to die.

Contemplating the decisions I've made in life, I'm not satisfied with the things that I've done.

I haven't lived. I haven't loved or felt valued and wanted.

I want that. I want to be something to someone. I want to be kissed passionately.

I really want to dance in the rain.

Princesses aren't allowed to dance in the rain. We could get sick, and no one likes a sick princess, or so I was told as a child. There's something about the idea of dancing out in a storm, holding my arms out and spinning round and round that I think would be so much fun.

Fun.

Princesses don't have fun either.

Too lost in thought and waiting for death, I'm only half aware of the thunderous bang that happens close enough that the ground beneath me shakes. Jostled by the sound I nearly open my eyes but then the Xaver shriek, reminding me to keep them closed.

Their collective, ear-piercing cries fill the night and the random roar that follows has me wish I *was* dead.

That wasn't the Xaver, I know it in my bones. The sound is too deep. Too mesmerising. That sound frightens me more than anything has in the last few hours of my terror-filled night.

The creatures touching me seem to evaporate like they weren't even there and I'm left hyperventilating on the ground, unsure what has just happened or what new monster is here ready to devour me.

That's when I feel it. Two large, masculine hands clutch either side of my face. I whimper against my closed mouth. My mind screams that I know who it is, but my body wont calm down.

It's not possible. He can't be here.

'Susyri, open your eyes Princess, you're safe. They're gone. I have you.'

I only comply because the way Zeke says princess is so different from the other times. Before it always had a hint of mockery. Now, he says it like an endearment.

When I manage to pry my lids open, I'm met with the face of my saviour. Only inches away from mine, Zeke hovers close. Those ever-green depths hold me tightly in their gaze. I see the anger lines in his brow. The worry etched into the firm set of his mouth. It all softens when I blink up at him, trying to process that he's here and that he is real.

For a moment, I think that maybe we've both died and we're in the afterlife. However, that would mean that we're both here together and that's a weird thought to have. He isn't my lover, or my family, which is the only way for us to be together in death.

I can't be dead anyway. If I was dead, my body wouldn't be throbbing in time to my heartbeat right now.

Searching my face, Zeke runs his thumb over my bottom lip, drawing me from my errant thoughts. The sting has me lick the spot he just touched. The metallic taste of blood hits my tongue and makes me wince. I must look a mess.

'I think I bit too hard trying not to make a noise,' I mutter, trying desperately to not lose the thin-layer of control I have left. I'm about to lose it. Tears are falling down my face and I fear that if I open my mouth again, I will break down.

Zeke begins to use his thumb to stroke up and down my jaw, in a soothing motion that has my composure crack.

'You did well, Susyri. You did really, really well.'

My chest swells and my stupid lip wobbles dramatically. His praise shifts something in me. 'I thought I was going to die. And I can't die yet, Zeke. I haven't danced in the rain. I haven't lived.' My voice is barely audible.

The tension leaves his face and with a small, barely-there smile, Zeke runs one hand down the side of my cheek. 'You want to dance in the rain, Princess?' he asks sweetly.

I nod, no longer fighting back the tears. 'Yes. And I want to eat one of those dishes with the raw meat that's cooked with citrus and no heat.'

Zeke's eyes are a brilliant green. So bright. So focused. He chuckles a breathy sound as if he has forgotten how to laugh. 'Are you sure? That dish doesn't taste very nice.'

'Princesses aren't allowed to eat raw food. No one wants a sick princess.'

I watch his brow furrow. 'Then we will dance in the rain and eat raw meat. I promise.'

Sniffling, I cry a little more. 'I thought I was going to die.'

Zeke opens and closes his mouth. My words have clearly affected him. 'I should've stayed with you. I'm sorry.'

Shaking my head, we haven't broken eye contact. His body is heavy against mine and it feels absolutely amazing. Instead of pain, I feel his warmth. 'You saved me, Zeke. You...how did you find me?' We had left him at the tavern, fighting a horde of Xaver. It doesn't make any sense.

'I told you I would,' is all he says and it's enough.

CHAPTER FORTY

'We need to go.'

Zeke's words remind me where we are and while I want to scream at him to come back when he pulls away and stands, I know we need to move. We're out in the open and only the Gods know what else is out there in the darkness. While I feel safe now that Zeke is with me, I don't want to tempt fate.

I take a moment to breathe and pull myself together. This is not the time to fall apart, even if all I want to do is curl into a ball and wail. I can't do that. I need to get over it. I've been through some shit and I have more to face, I can't let this deter me.

With every intention of jumping to my feet and focusing, the moment I try to sit, I cry an involuntary sound and flop back down against the littered forest floor. Zeke's warmth kept the pain away and now, I'm left, unable to move. It feels like every inch of me has taken a beating.

Zeke is there in an instant. 'Why didn't you tell me you were hurt! Where is the pain?'

I have no idea why he's so angry.

'Everywhere.'

The way he cusses has me blush and before I can tell him to just give me a moment before I try and rise again, he bends and scoops me up.

I yelp in surprise.

Wide eyed, my attention snaps to his face and I instinctively wrap my arms around his neck to hold on.

My body curls into his chest. I relax into his hold, grateful that I don't have to walk. Grateful that I can take some time to fully compose myself.

'Thank you,' I whisper, unable to stop studying his perfect jawline and the way his hair moves in the light breeze.

Zeke's eyes are dark, almost black, and while I know it's probably a trick of the darkness surrounding us, it holds my attention. This man makes me feel things I've never felt before. It's confusing.

'You're welcome,' he replies smoothly. It takes a few heartbeats for me to process what he has just said and the way in which he says it. I cackle. All the tension in my body evaporates and I bury my head into his neck and breathe him in. Tears fall down my face and I laugh despite everything.

'You're such an ass,' I tell his shoulder and feel his body vibrate slightly against mine. I look up sharply to catch him laughing and glare up at the man who is focusing on the path we are taking. Not a hint of humour on his face, except the lines around his eyes. 'I guess I owe you now.'

That has his attention briefly fall to my face. Gods he's gorgeous. 'I guess you do.'

I have an overwhelming need to kiss him. To feel those lips on mine.

'Oh thank the heavens!' The voice snaps me from my silly thoughts and I'm overwhelmed with guilt when I gasp and turn to see Henry, Fi and Calligan all bloodied and smiling on the road.

I forgot about them.

Shame has me smiling weakly at Henry as he rushes over. He takes in the way Zeke holds me and what I can only assume, the atrocious way I look. 'It's so good to see you well, Betty.'

'You too, Henry,' I reply weakly, feeling horrible. 'Is everyone all right? Is Burk here? Is he okay?' Scanning the crew, I notice him by the horses. I can't see any obvious missing limbs.

'All is well, Lady. Zeke rescued Burk, got to us in time, and I see he found you too. The hero of the night.'

Stunned by that piece of information, I stare up at the stoic face of the male holding me.

'It's another life debt I owe him,' Henry states, his tone hard to decipher.

Zeke grunts and heads straight for Horse and Toppin, clearly not in the mood for conversation. 'We move out,' he instructs, not waiting to see if the others will follow. He gently lifts me onto Horse's saddle and jumps up behind me. His thick arms cage me on either side, holding me in place.

'I can ride,' I say weakly and get a grunt in return. It makes me smile.

Zeke holds Horse's reins firmly and kicks the beast into getting us as far from the road as possible.

CHAPTER FORTY ONE

Over the last few hours of riding, I have silently wept, gotten angry to the point of fearing my heart would stop beating, worried over realising that the world is full of monsters, and then accepted that I took this quest knowing that I could die at any moment.

All this between dozing in and out of sleep, snuggly within Zeke's embrace.

We ride all night and only stop when the sun begins to rise.

Zeke leads us to a secluded, grassy flat spot next to a river. We're off the Tilman Road for now.

Zeke gets off Horse, and without a word, lifts me out of the saddle and carries me over to the trunk of an ancient oak.

Placing me down gently, he looks deep in thought as he fusses around, gathering branches and making a fire.

The water flows a few paces away and Henry and the others silently work alongside my companion. Fi is limping and I feel instantly bad for sitting on my butt while they do all the work.

However, when I go to stand with the intent of helping, I receive a mighty glare from the man now building up the flames of the firepit.

Conceding, I raise my hands in submission and sit back down. Gods, he's in a mood and while I'd normally love to poke him to get a reaction, however, something in me screams to just be good.

For now.

Besides, he did save my life, which has been playing around in my head over and over. I vaguely remember the rumble of the earth under me as something struck the ground and I can't be certain, but that frightening growl didn't sound like a noise a man could make. It sounded animalistic. Predatory.

Gods, I probably made the entire thing up in my head. I was on my back, covered in eyeball-eating tiny monsters, so I think I can give myself a little grace period.

Watching Zeke move that powerful body of his around the camp, I try to piece together everything that happened and am left with a throbbing pain between my ears. There are just too many questions. *How did he get to me so fast when we rode on horseback, at speed, away from where we left him? How was he able to defeat the Xavar? Why did Henry leave him behind and have so much faith that Zeke could kill mythical, human eating creatures?*

Zeke silently stomps over to the river, fills a bowl with water, stomps over to Horse, grabs something from his bag, and then storms over to me. He places the bowl down beside my leg and then asks me to show him my hands. I do obediently and realise that the skin is all shredded and bloody.

He makes a funny noise that captures my attention and I look up sharply to try and work out what I just heard. He isn't looking at me though. His ever-green eyes are set on my injuries.

Slowly, he begins to wipe my wounds and the memory of the last time we were in this position replays in my mind. With each stroke of the water-soaked cloth, I contemplate all that has happened and all that has changed in the short amount of time that I've met him.

With my right palm in his hand and his attention on me, I fight with the growing need to bombard him with all my questions. To ask him why he is doing this. Why he is helping and risking his life for me.

The words don't come. They get stuck in my throat. The pain in my palms slowly recedes and I comply when he asks to see my other injuries.

Zeke doesn't say a word when I have to lift the cloth of my ripped pants to show him my damaged knees. He just shakes his head like he's annoyed and begins to tend to them as well.

The noise of the camp fades away until there is just him and I. He is so close that all I can smell is him. So close that I could reach out and brush away the soft brown hair that has fallen around his face as he works.

'You don't have to. I can do it.'

'I want to,' is his snapped out response.

Confused, I ask him why he's angry and then gape when he says, 'because I should've been there. You should never have been hurt.'

'Zeke you're not responsible for me.'

'Am I not?' he asks, raising a brow at me in challenge. I don't know what to say. Something is different between us.

Shaking his head, Zeke goes back to fixing me up. 'You handled yourself very well out there, Princess. You're strong and brave. A warrior.'

I snort. 'I'm a bastard princess, Zeke. I'm no one.'

He doesn't seem very impressed. 'You're wrong. You're not no one, Susyri. And I'd love to get my hands on the people that made you feel like you were.'

Staring, we both seem lost in each other's eyes. I watch as those magnificent depths fall to my lips and back, so unbelievable slowly. His energy draws me in, and no longer able to fight it, I lean forward when he does.

We spring apart just before our lips touch at the sound of Henry calling out to inform us that some food has been prepared.

Awkwardly, I look anywhere but at the man I nearly kissed.

Zeke busies himself with collecting the bowl. There is a part of me that wants him to stop and finish what we were about to do. Another part tells me to not be so silly. I don't know him. It's been a handful of days.

What is wrong with me?

'I'll get you something to eat. Rest here.' I watch as his gaze flicks to the space between my breasts and I quickly look down to see that the emerald has slipped from under my tunic. It's on full display.

Zeke's face hardens before he walks away leaving me wanting to shout at him to come back.

CHAPTER FORTY TWO

Everyone spends the morning cleaning their wounds and relaxing. I manage to get an hour or so of sleep against the tree and have been sitting in the same spot, trying to not ogle the male now bathing in the river.

Calligan and Burk are with Zeke, their tunics off and their hair glistens in the sun. All three men are exceptionally built, making me question what they do in life. Only one has my full attention though. The one who I was sure was going to kiss me this morning.

Zeke has a body like no one I've ever seen, and I have seen a great deal of shirt-less men in the training yards at the castle. His abdomen is defined in an eight pack. The hardness and the way it appears to be painted on, makes me subtly check if I'm drooling. His arms are thick and bulging.

I shiver, remembering the way he carried me. How those arms caged me on horseback last night. The curves that dip down into his trousers has me fan myself against the heat of the morning. I can't help but imagine where the lines lead.

A dangerous thought. Something I shouldn't be doing and yet...I can't help myself. When we first met, I thought he was an arrogant pig. A drifter on the Tilman Road. Now...well, now, I still think he's pretty arrogant, but he's also strong and unwavering. Gentle and protective.

'You look better,' Henry says, appearing beside me. I shuffle over so that he can sit down. He does so with a small grunt.

Henry was injured pretty badly on the hip. The bruise is massive. They all did a bit of an assessment of their wounds after Zeke made sure I was okay.

Fi has a number of cuts and what appeared to be a bite on her thigh that I think will give me nightmares for the rest of my life.

Burk and Calligan got pretty beat up. Calligan has a large gash on the side of his face, very close to his eye and Burk looks like he went three rounds with a giant and lost. Everyone is alive though.

I have no idea what Henry wants when he asks me how I'm 'holding up.'

'I'm okay,' I reply absently. I'd be better if he left me alone so that I could stare at Zeke a little more.

Right now, I have to pretend that I was observing the pretty environment. It's actually a nice spot compared to the other places I've had to stay in along this damn road.

'I'm glad to hear that, Princess.'

My stomach drops into my butt.

Attention snapping to the man beside me, I find it hard to draw in enough air. Henry is staring at me like he's assessing my reaction, and stupid me, has only just realised that I've given everything away.

Every muscle in my body tenses.

Henry must see it because he grips my arm, keeping me from jumping up. I don't know how to react to this.

'I don't know—'

'Come on, *Betty*. I heard what Zeke called you last night, *Susi*. You don't need to fear me. I'll keep your secret.' Henry's tone leaves no room for me to deny him. He clearly has worked it out and still, knowing who I am, he helped. He hasn't tried to steal me away to hand me over for some kind of reward...yet.

I sit back a little, no longer feeling the need to escape. 'Why would you keep who I am to yourself? There's a big reward for my head, dead or alive, or so I've been told.'

Henry huffs what I can only assume is a laugh. 'I do not care for any reward. You're under Zeke's protection, which means I will not betray you.'

That catches my attention and I draw my gaze from the man still bathing in the water.

'He really means that much to you? The Queen wants my head, Henry. You should use it. You'd be a very rich man.'

Henry clicks his tongue as if I've said the silliest thing in the world. 'Zeke has saved my life countless times over the last five years. Yesterday is just another debt I owe him. My job puts me in many dangerous situations.'

'You said you were a merchant,' I state, only just realising that Henry and his crew are far from what they've told me. They're probably criminals. Which would mean that Zeke is probably just like them.

Not that it matters.

Leaning forward, I pull my legs up and hug them.

Henry is watching the same show I am, except I don't think it's for the same reasons. 'I'm a little confused though. Zeke is not someone to attach himself to anyone, especially a woman.'

Gods. 'Thanks,' I huff. *What does that even mean?*

Henry chuckles. 'I didn't mean it to come out like that. I meant that in all my time, I haven't seen him care this much.'

That catches my attention. 'What do you mean?'

'I mean that Zeke is a free spirit. A loner.'

Studying the guy in the water a little more, I listen intently. 'Do you know anything about his history?'

'Not much. He isn't known for being a talker. All I know is that Zeke was destined to be a leader amongst his people and he lost his way. He doesn't see his greatness like we do. He's a gift to anyone who knows him.'

I don't know what exactly Henry has just said that makes the hair on my body stand on end.

I shiver.

Silently we sit, both of us lost in our thoughts, until I shift my position and then hear Henry gasp lightly.

'What?' I question, sitting up quickly.

Gaze snapping to the man beside me, I realise he is staring at my chest.

I slowly follow his line of sight to the jewel that has fallen between the buttons of the new tunic I put on earlier.

The emerald seems to wink as the light catches it and I quickly shove it back under my shirt and sit up.

We don't say anything for a long moment and I shuffle against the hard ground at being studied so intensely.

Henry opens and closes his mouth a few times. Shakes his head a bit. He finally states, 'I don't know what you're doing out here on the Tilman Road, Princess Susyri, but I'm glad that you're with someone like Zeke. I was unsure why my friend was taking such an interest in matters of the crown, but I understand now. I wish you all the happiness. Be assured that your secret is safe with me.' I watch Henry rise, he bows deeply when he stands and then leaves me to my raging thoughts.

Knowing I'm being watched, I look over at the river and collide with the colour of ever-green.

CHAPTER FORTY THREE

After the conversation with Henry, I keep my distance from the rest of the group for the remainder of the day. I take my time caring for Toppin and Horse.

Something Henry said disturbed me and I keep checking the emerald under my tunic, like I'm expecting it to disappear. I've also made a point of keeping away from Zeke.

I'm disorientated and confused. My body is still sore.

Sitting back against the tree, I study the environment feeling a deep sense of disquiet. I've been on this road for weeks and I've noticed a significant change in the nature around the road. I haven't had a true moment to sit and actually absorb that information. There is a denseness to the forest here. A darkness that sends a chill up my spine.

The others have started to make the evening meal. Zeke and Calligan have only just come back from hunting and there are a few rabbits on the fire. Fi is pulling fruit and wrapped bread from their bags.

The thought of eating has me sick to my stomach. I offered to help but Fi just told me to rest. Worried that she knows who I truly am and that is the reason she has declined my assistance, I've stayed away and chosen not to push it.

I don't have the energy to do anything but sit in my own misery. The events from last night seem to have caught up with me.

We were attacked by Xaver.

Xaver.

I heard people die. I heard noises that will haunt me forever and it doesn't seem like such a big deal. I had to be blindfolded so that I wasn't murdered by tiny eye-ball eating creatures that I naively believed were myth. There's a very large part of me that wishes I could go back to that little bubble of ignorance.

It makes me question everything.

Like, what other otherworldly beings actually exist and am I going to face any more as I continue on this quest.

Heaven knows what will be in the Dead Forest.

I was useless in the tavern. I had to be carried from the place and did nothing to help. I knew that my chances of surviving this were slim but now it seems impossible. Death is coming for me, I know it now. I just hope I can save my father before that happens.

Feeling sorry for myself, I can't stop the raging, negative thoughts replaying in my mind. It's just an endless series of 'why's'. *Why did my mother have to die? Why do I have to be the bastard princess? Why did that lady, the 'messenger', have to give me such a dangerous and unrealistic quest? Why does the Queen have to hate me so much?*

Gripping my head, I practically pull at my hair to try to stop the voices in my head. Especially the voice of the messenger who seems to be the loudest. *Follow the Tilman Road until you reach the Dead Forest, find the gift returned and get past the monster that guards the road out. Get to the top of Ekalus Peak. Only then will you be granted an audience with the Alpha Lord. When you are there, tell him your story, tell him of your lineage and what has happened here tonight. Show him the emerald and ask for his blood.*

Why did I listen?

There is also the other issue of Zeke. He could have died last night helping me. What if he doesn't want to stay with me.

I wouldn't.

Why would he risk his life for me, and my quest, to find the Alpha Lord?

Tears prickle the corner of my eyes and I roughly wipe them away. I was a fool to think that I could do this. I'm just a bastard princess, with minimal training and a life that isn't my own.

I want to scream.

I'm fucking betrothed.

I'm so messed up that I pushed that piece of information to the back of my mind and every time it pops up, I kick it back in its corner. I don't have time to worry about what will happen if I ever get back to the castle. After last night, I seriously don't think I will.

Zeke slumps down beside me, pushing me from my thoughts. I keep my head down and my hands pulling at my hair. I don't want him to see my tears. I'm a mess.

'Here,' he states, dropping a plate of bread and rabbit at my feet.

'Thank you. I just need a moment on my own.'

Gods, I'm pathetic.

'I don't know what's going through your head, but you need to eat.'

'I'm not hungry,' I reply a little petulantly, drawing my knees up and hugging them in a feeble attempt at finding comfort. Resting my chin against my knees, I don't know if I want him to go away or stay. Which just makes me feel even more confused. 'I guess I'm not as strong as you thought, hey.'

'Just eat,' Zeke demands, not acknowledging what I've said. A piece of flatbread wrapped meat appears in my line of vision.

'Zeke,' I grumble and then sigh heavily when he tells me that he will feed me like a child if I don't put the piece in my mouth. I reluctantly take it with a scowl and chew away. It actually tastes really good, and I feel instantly better. 'Do you know that Henry knows who I am?'

'Yeah, that big bastard is smarter than he looks.'

Frowning, I'm not sure why I'm so angry all of a sudden. 'Why do you sound so calm?'

He shrugs and I want to smack him. And I also want to shuffle closer to his warmth and breathe in that masculine, sinful scent. Damn him. Damn my thoughts and damn this quest!

'Because it doesn't matter, princess. Henry is loyal. He won't tell your secrets.' Here he goes, back to making the word princess sound like an insult.

'He told me.' Gods, I sound so awkward.

I feel awkward. We nearly kissed.

We sit in silence, listening to the others chatting and laughing. 'Eat some more. It'll make you feel better. You've been through a massive ordeal.'

Sitting up, I concede and grab some more food from my plate. It's making me feel a lot better having food to focus on. Zeke watches me and thankfully doesn't say a word.

'Did you eat?' I question and frown when he shakes his head. I offer him the plate and try to decipher the expression that flashes over his face.

'It's your food, Princess. You have it. I'll be fine.'

Rolling my eyes, I shove it towards him like he did to me. 'Just take some. Please, for me.'

Frowning, he does, and for some reason it makes me happy. That's when I realise my mind is quiet, that Zeke has chased the negative thoughts away.

CHAPTER FORTY FOUR

'Zeke, how did you know about the Xaver? And why did the others look to you for all the answers?' The questions spill out of me before I can contain them.

'When you've been on the road as long as I have, you see and experience things.' His tone makes me pause. I busy myself eating some more and making sure that Zeke is taking some too. It feels nice to eat together like this.

'How long have you been on the road?'

He appears to be only a few years older than me. I blame Henry for my curiosity.

'Longer than I care to admit,' he replies solemnly.

'What about your family?' I've tried to ask him before about his life and he's always been so evasive. Henry said he was supposed to be a leader which means his family must have some kind of influence in whatever province he is from.

'I left a long time ago, after a falling-out with my father.

I lost someone close to me, and for many years I was a shell of what I once was. My father wanted me to take over the family business and wanted me to move-on. I wasn't interested. It turned into a big thing.'

Shrugging those wide shoulders, Zeke seems to realise how much he has disclosed and I realise that my mouth had fallen open at some point during his speech. I clap it back shut.

'Was it a family member or friend that you lost?' I remember the pain when my mother died. I thought I'd never feel whole, never laugh, or find happiness in the world again.

'My brother,' he offers and I genuinely have no idea why he is telling me this. The way he says it has me swallow the next question.

'I'm so sorry.'

Zeke leaves the last bit of food and picks up the plate to offer it to me. 'Eat the rest.'

'I'm not—'

'You need your strength, Susi. We leave early tomorrow morning to visit the last town on the Tilman Road before we get to the Dead Forest. Eat.'

I do. 'Thank you. For everything, Zeke. Also…after last night, you don't have to…you don't…' Gods, why is it so hard to tell him that he doesn't have to come with me. Probably because I want him to.

'Susi,' Zeke states in a tone that has me look up at him. 'There is nothing that could stop me going with you the rest of the way. Our journeys are interwoven and I won't leave you.'

Gods.

Rising, with the intent of finding Toppin and making sure he is all right, I stop and press a kiss to his cheek. I don't know why I do it. I just wanted to. 'I'm lucky to have met you, Zeke.'

I feel his gaze as I walk away.

CHAPTER FORTY FIVE

Later that night, I snuggle within my bedroll beside my tree and try to not imagine pixie-monsters coming from the forest. It's a useless endeavour. All I hear is tapping and I swear there is something running around out there in the darkness.

Logically, I know that I'm okay and safe. I've been told that two people are going to be up on watch throughout the night.

I apparently can't be trusted to have a watch. Or at least that is how I felt after I was told no.

All that information still doesn't help me to relax enough to close my eyes.

Fearing that I won't be able to get a wink of sleep, I turn over and find someone standing over me. I watch, in silence, as Zeke lays out his bedroll and lowers himself into it.

He gets comfortable, moves around a bit and then calms.

Now on my back, staring at the star-covered sky, we lay shoulder-to-shoulder.

'I don't think I'm going to be able to sleep,' I confess to the stars.

'I don't blame you. Your first experience with the Xaver leaves an impact.' Zeke moves his arm above my head and after a moment of awkward staring at it, I watch his face as I lift my head slowly and bite my sore lip when he lowers it down so that I'm using his arm as a pillow.

His warmth hits me instantly. The smell of him hits next, and it's intoxicating.

Zeke's staring and as if hesitating, he curls his arm, drawing me into his side. Every muscle tenses as my front touches his body. It's a lot. He is…a lot. I'm all stiff and unmoving.

Not sure where to put my limbs, I tuck my arms around my middle and keep my legs straight, when all I want to do is throw them over his solid form.

A large hand lands on my back and begins to slowly move along my spine. I relax with each stroke.

A small noise to my left has me look over quickly in fright.

'It's only Calligan and Fi,' Zeke reassures me, squeezing me briefly.

I watch them head into the trees. 'What are they doing?'

'What do you think?'

Confused, I confess, 'I genuinely have no idea.'

Zeke laughs softly and shakes his head. 'They're taking a moment for some *alone* time.'

'I'm lost. Why would they want alone time?' It's dark in the trees. What could they possibly want to do out there?

'Sex, Susyri.'

Oh. 'Uhhh, right.' Gods, I'm daft. I didn't even realise they were together.

We slip into an awkward silence. I become very aware of my body touching his like saying the word, 'sex', has put ideas into my head. Ideas that have been there for a while now, if I'm honest.

'Did I make you uncomfortable?' He sounds amused and I quickly snap a, 'no! I know what…I don't need…I didn't realise they were…you know…that's all.' The horde of Xaver could come from the trees right now and I'd let them take me.

Zeke laughs a deep sound that vibrates against my body.

'Don't laugh at me!' I demand.

Sitting up, I stare in wonder at the male who can't seem to contain himself. Zeke's laughter does something to my soul. Watching his face lit up with humour softens his hard, masculine features.

He holds his chest and wipes his face, all whilst I gape at him in wonder. He just keeps going and I find myself drawn into his energy. My giggles come out of nowhere and I leave him to it and lay back down. He can laugh at me all he likes if it brings him joy.

'I'm not laughing at you,' he finally says, once he gets himself under control. 'It's just the look on your face was priceless.'

'Wow, thanks. I'm glad my face makes you laugh.' I'm not serious, he can laugh at my face all he likes if he continues to make that noise.

Gripping my chin softly, Zeke lifts my face so that my attention is on him. 'You're the most gorgeous female I have ever met, Princess.'

Holy heavens! I forget to breathe. To think. To close my mouth as it hangs open while staring at his hand-crafted face.

Locked in his gaze, the world slips away. There's a moment where I believe we will finally have that kiss.

A moment that passes when he says, 'I haven't laughed like that in a long time, thank you.'

'You laugh at me all the time,' I grumble and lay back down on his arm. Damn fool has been laughing since I met him. He is right though. I haven't heard him laugh like *that* before.

'True. You are very funny.'

I'm falling for him. In a way that I shouldn't be. From the games we played when we first met, to me being here wrapped against him. It feels like I've known him forever, not a handful of days. The problem is, technically, even though I haven't agreed, I am betrothed. However, I did almost die last night. While a lot of what happened is a blur of fear in my mind, I remember fixating on the idea that I haven't lived.

Fiddling with the stone under my shirt, I draw his attention.

Zeke doesn't hesitate as he grabs the chain around my neck and lifts it. He holds up the emerald so that we're both staring at it. The chain is long enough to not be uncomfortable. It feels weird not having its warm surface touching my skin. I've gotten so used to it.

'Why do you think I have to show this to the Alpha Lord?' It is a question I've been contemplating for a while now. It's odd that someone who, if the stories are correct, holds immense power, would be swayed by a jewel. Yes, it's massive and very rare, but it doesn't really make sense.

'Objects can have meaning and influence,' Zeke replies as if his thoughts are a million miles away.

He touches the green surface with a single finger.

'I guess.' I'm not very convinced.

He must sense that because he elaborates by explaining, 'think of objects like crowns. Your father is King and I could pass him in the streets and have no idea who he is. If he wore his crown, people would instantly recognise the meaning.'

His brow is furrowed as he moves the stone back and forward as if waiting for it to tell him something.

'That makes sense. Though, what an emerald could be a symbol for is hard to imagine.'

'Stones hold power. They're of this earth.'

He sounds like he knows what he's talking about. 'It is beautiful though. I love how it catches the light and how it feels warm against my skin.'

Zeke lowers the stone and I grab it and place it back under my shirt, feeling more comfortable with it on my skin. Confusion crests his features. 'It's warm?'

'Yeah,' I manage to get out through a wide yawn.

Zeke chuckles to himself and pulls me harder to his side. I snuggle close to the heat of his body and feel my lids grow heavy. 'Sleep, Princess. Nothing will harm you whilst I'm here.'

'I know,' I mumble just as I give into the pull of oblivion.

I dream of his lips brushing against my forehead.

I fall asleep easily with the simple thought that I am safe within Zeke's embrace.

CHAPTER FORTY SIX

'Good morning.' My greeting is awkward. I'm the last to be ready and find a spot beside the small fire. The others have already started breaking their fast. There are three more rabbits on the fire and there are breads, fruits and nuts. It's definitely more than what I was eating while I was traveling on my own.

Zeke looks up from his plate and nods in my direction by way of greeting. His bright green eyes travel up and down my body before he goes back to his food.

I feel my face heat and subtly run my hand through the long strands of my hair. I threw on the only clean, unripped pair of brown traveling pants I had and a cream tunic that I have to pull over my head. The emerald sits heavily around my neck under it.

He held me all night. When I woke he was gone though.

'Good morning, Princess,' Henry drawls from across the fire.

I falter, unsure what to do or say. He just called me princess in front of everyone. Henry just keeps grinning while I slowly look around to see everyone's reaction and observe their bored, uninterested features.

'Relax, Your Highness, your secret is out and it matters not to us if you are Betty Colt, the wife of Zeke, or a Lady of the Ekalus'

I shiver at that and sit. 'Gods, could you imagine being a Lady of the Ekalus? Can you imagine how frightening an Ekalus would be, especially after the Xaver last night?'

I'm not sure what has Henry throw his head back and howl in laughter or what has Zeke glare at him from where he sits to the right of the flames. Fi just shakes her head and hands me a plate.

'What did I say?' I ask her quietly.

'Nothing, My Lady.'

Bristling at the title, I take the plate. 'Please, I'm a bastard. There's no need to speak to me so formally. Call me Susi.'

'Good,' Burk says from across the fire. His tone leaves nothing to the imagination of how he feels about the crown.

Zeke makes a funny noise that has Burk shut his mouth and continue to eat.

'It's okay,' I venture. 'You don't have to like me or my family. I do really appreciate you all keeping my secret though.'

'We aren't doing it for you. We do it for—'

'If you are doing it for me,' Zeke cuts the hairy man off, his voice full of rage. 'Then you would know the way you're speaking to Susi right now *is* disrespecting me. You will watch your tone when you address her.'

I shut my mouth and hang my head, mostly to cover the fact that my face is all red. I know I must be the colour of a beetroot.

Zeke is furious, and while he doesn't raise his voice, the threat and command in what he's saying is enough to have everyone stop eating and for Burk to look somewhat contrite.

'Please, we're all friends here,' Henry proclaims, his tone light and cheerful. 'Burk means no disrespect. Do you Burk?' While he is being chirpy, even I can hear the warning in Henry's tone now.

I feel the tension leave the campfire as Burk nods and apologises.

'Forgive us, Susi,' Fi says. 'Life out here is tough and there is not much love for the crown. The nobles of this kingdom have done nothing for my brother and I. We have struggled every day of our lives.'

'I understand,' I reply softly. 'I don't expect you to treat me any differently, but I would hope that you'd wait and make your own judgement on me as a person, and not who my father is. Give me that chance before you decide whether you like me or not, please.'

My speech has everyone staring. I even see a spark of respect from Burk as he bows his head. 'You're right. Our father was an abusive arsehole who ran out on us when we were young. No one deserves to be judged by the actions of their parents. I am sorry, Susi.'

I look at Fi and Burk a little differently now and know they don't need my sympathy over what he has just said. I just reply with, 'Thank you Burk.'

Zeke nods in my direction and the conversation around the fire becomes a little more comfortable.

Until Henry says, 'so, the Dead Forest huh?'

CHAPTER FORTY SEVEN

It's been a massive day and it's gone by in a blur of activity.

We arrived in the town of Frycinta around mid-afternoon. It's the biggest town on the Tilman Road, and the busiest.

Trust my luck that we arrived on market day. The streets were packed and while I was in a group, I found myself constantly trying to stay beside Zeke.

It could've been my imagination but I felt that he was doing the same. At one point when I got separated while buying some supplies for our trek into the Dead Forest, I found my way back to them only because Zeke was shouting my fake name in the crowd. It was loud and a bit much, but also heart-warming.

I did get in trouble for wandering off like a child, which killed that buzz. Actually, it didn't. It just emphasised how much he cares.

My feelings for Zeke have grown so much in the last few days. The intensity of them is hard to process.

'Eat and drink up, Betty, who knows when your next hot meal will be after tomorrow!' A plate and mug of ale is placed down in front of me. My thanks is drowned out by the volume of chatting in the tavern we're staying in tonight. Another storm swept through the lands, bringing with it more lightning and thunder. We are only half a day's ride or so from the Dark Forest and Henry clearly doesn't realise the impact his words have on my nerves.

If I have to hear one more comment about Zeke and I heading into the next part of our journey tomorrow, I might just scream.

The others offered to come with us but Zeke made it clear that he didn't want any more people to look after. It was a snide comment that had me glaring at him for half our shopping trip, not that it seemed to faze him. At least I know that everything that has happened over the last two days hasn't changed his personality.

'Leave her alone, Hen,' Fi defends with a mouthful of food. Burt and Calligan are busy eating and don't pay Henry any attention.

'I'm only teasing,' he retorts, throwing me a wink. He sits down across from me and starts eating his meal.

I tuck into my own hot bowl of pastry topped stew. It's like a pie without the bottom and it's really good.

Not realising how hungry I was, I finish half the meal in a couple of bites. Downing my ale, I soak up the atmosphere in this new tavern.

The place is bigger than the others I've stayed at, much like the town. It's probably housing nearly two hundred patrons right now. It's loud, full of energy and noise, and a great place to be when you want to stay inconspicuous.

Would've been even better if all of the places I've stayed at were like this. I wouldn't have had all the trouble that I did along this Gods-forsaken road.

Finishing the pie and ale, Henry offers me more from the massive jug.

'I probably shouldn't,' I start and then nod when Henry tells me that I will be heading into a place called the Dead Forest tomorrow and that I should live a little before I do. 'You're right. Fill it up, Hen!'

'That's the spirit,' he exclaims and tops his own up in the process. The others are chatting away down the other side of the table. Zeke is in a deep discussion with Fi and Burk about roads and tales they've heard about the Dead Forest. No one has been in there, clearly. It's giving me anxiety just hearing some of their words.

'Don't pay too much attention to it. You and Zeke will be fine.'

'I hope so.' I sigh, throwing another glance in Zeke's direction. He's risking so much coming with me. 'Is it selfish for me to ask him to come along?' I ask, genuinely unsure what I should do.

The deep frown on Henry's face changes his energy. 'I'm afraid he wouldn't listen if you told him to stay.' He's probably right.

'That doesn't make me feel any better.'

'I know. However, you and Zeke are on the same path now. Your fates are intertwined.'

Smiling up at him, I take another big gulp.

Heat fills my body, making me feel all light as I finish the mug. Henry fills it again instantly.

'That was very wise,' I tell him, watching the froth form on the top of my refilled drink.

Grinning like a fool, Henry catches up to me by downing his full mug and re-filling it. 'I can be very philosophical when I want to be.'

'You sure can.' Another mug gone. Henry is right, I could be dead tomorrow and this is the best tasting ale I've ever had.

Feeling a little light-heated and hot, I snort-laugh at the man who finds it hilarious how fast I can knock back a drink. We both finish our next round with a small competition that I lose.

I'm a close second though.

Having fun with Henry, I eat another plate of food and share another jug of alcohol, all the while soaking in the life around me. My last night of fun.

A performer that I recognise from a few nights back steps into the middle of the room with his band behind him. The strum of the first strings of a lute fills the tavern and I squeak in excitement. Henry finds that very amusing and we both turn our attention to the bard who starts singing his ballad.

CHAPTER FORTY EIGHT

'I'll tell you a tale, a tale of old,
Where the wings didn't scare you,
And the women were bold.
Where a beast of the sky,
Was every lover's dream,
And being alone was the reason to die.
You see,
An Ekalus is a one-woman show,
A love for the ages,
A stone he'd bestow.
A treasure that marks,
A soul with a soul,
A stone to bind two hearts,
It is their ultimate goal.
For only a pair,

> *can make two a three,*
> *And that is where fate is not fair,*
> *A rare gift is an Ekalus babe-ee.*
>
> *But beware,*
> *Sweet audience,*
> *For the stories are true,*
> *Death will be waiting,*
> *If you touch a heartstone,*
> *That is not meant for you.'*

There's a long pause in the tavern as the ballad comes to an end. The storyteller's words bounce around in my ale-muddled head and I clap when the rest of the patrons find their way out of the trance his beautiful voice seemed to put everyone in. Applauding along with me, Henry throws me a wink when I exclaim how impressed I am at this entertainer.

'I'd love to get him to come play for my father,' I say, a little too loudly. 'He loves a good storyteller. Dancing too. My father loves dancing. I think it is where I get it from.' Henry's face lights up as if he has an idea and he springs out of his chair with a little wobble. I guess the ale is affecting him as much as it is me. 'We shall dance. That's what you need tonight, My Lady.'

He's off, heading towards the musicians who take his coin and begin to prepare themselves. Watching with a giggle as Henry finds his way back, I take his hand when he bows and offers it. Music has erupted in the tavern and I'm thrilled to see we aren't the only ones pairing off to dance.

Henry leads me to the makeshift dancefloor and swings me around. It feels so good to move and let go.

Time has no meaning when you're drinking and dancing. At one point we end up in a line-dance with the locals, learning a quick-step jig that has tears run down my face from laughter.

Back in Henry's arms, I'm so unaware of what is happening around me that I'm not ready when Zeke appears. All of a sudden, I'm sandwiched between the man I'm dancing with and the man I'm trying to ignore. Peeking up through my squashed position, I catch the look that passes over Henry's face at whatever Zeke is now saying to him. I can't hear a thing, the music and noise around us is too loud. Henry looks behind his shoulder and all the humour falls from his face. He nods. Zeke nods. I think I ask them what is happening, but I must only say it in my head, because they don't acknowledge me. Then Henry spins me into Zeke's arms and heads into the crowd.

'Is everything okay?' I enquire, maybe slurring one or two words.

Zeke's ever-green depths fall to my face as he envelopes me in his embrace. 'Everything's fine. I just wanted to dance with my wife.' He is lying. I'm drunk, so...I don't care.

'You know how to dance?'

A sound comes from deep in his chest, then I'm dancing with Zeke and it's so much *more* than being in Henry's arms.

CHAPTER FORTY NINE

It's late and I'm not able to walk straight by the time Zeke escorts me up to the room we apparently 'have to share' tonight. Henry and the others walk us up to the door and if the room would stop spinning, I'd be able to work out why everyone is acting so weird.

I originally had my own room. I open my mouth to go to ask why things have changed about three times and forget how to form a sentence.

I snort-laugh when I go to talk again and say, 'what says us on the tomorrow.'

Burk snorts. 'I think it's time you found your bed.'

Calligan shakes his head and leads Fi to the top level of the tavern.

I think Henry tells me to go to sleep well before he too disappears.

Zeke leans over where I'm resting against the wall to open our door. That's when I notice someone down the hall. Before I can focus my attention, which is very hard to do right now, Zeke pulls me into the room.

About to tell him that I think I saw Captain Jorge, I notice the bed and realise how tired I am. Every other thought evaporates because right now, I need to go to sleep.

Flopping down on top of the comforter, I'm very impressed with how much bigger this room is to the last one we shared.

The large window across from the bed gives us a big show of the storm outside and I kick off my shoes and pull off my tunic. The emerald slaps against my chest and I tuck it under the material covering my breasts. My shirt flies across the room.

I need to be comfortable. I need to sleep.

I need food.

'I'm hungry,' I announce and slip under the covers once I get my trousers off and throw them too.

Snuggling against the scratchy sheet, I grumble, 'what I would do for a soft bed. Out of all the luxuries back in the castle, I miss that the most.'

Zeke makes a weird sound that has me blink towards where I think he is. I can't be sure if he's picking up my clothes because everything is all blurry and rotating.

'I don't feel well,' I state, not able to catch the groan as I try to roll over.

'That doesn't surprise me, you and Henry drank half the bar. Sleep, Princess. We leave early in the morning.'

I don't know what I say next. It makes Zeke laugh that chesty sound though.

Smiling, I fall to sleep.

Rousing, I swallow the acid-y bile in the back of my throat and curse my life. I feel really bad. My head is pounding and I blink over at the window and see two large figures.

One is standing inside the room and the other on the other side of the window. Which is how I know I'm seeing things. We're three storey's high.

Reaching over, I feel the warmth of Zeke on the sheets and am comforted by the fact. Closing my lids to stop the pain behind them is the only way I can think to make myself feel better.

It's still dark outside and the storm is raging, so I turn over and fall back asleep with two men talking in my head. It's a weird dream. A drunk dream that haunts me through the night.

'This is the closest you have ever been to home, Ezekiel. Does that mean you're coming back?' the deep voice from outside says. The sound of it sends a chill down my spine.

'You know I can't go back, Luke. The Alpha made it clear that if I step back on territory grounds, that I would not be leaving again. That it would be me accepting my role.' I feel like I know that voice, though it sounds off. Covered in power. More otherworldly.

'And that is a bad thing, my friend?'

'I'm not ready. It should have been Abe.'

'Yes, it should've been. But Abe is no longer of this world. You need to heal that pain. It's been too long.'

'I should've been with him that day.'

'But you weren't, and that is life. Throwing your stone away and leaving was not the way to handle it. Your parents were gifted two younglings, when younglings are so rare amongst our race. Now they've lost them both. One to an accident of fate and the other to grief. How do you think they feel?'

'Do we have to have this conversation again? I would like to get back to my bed.'

'A bed you are sharing with whom? Is that the reason you are so close to our lines?'

'She's nobody, Luke. Just a body to warm my bed for the night. Now, leave me to my business. Stay out of my way.'

'Is that a command from my future Alpha?'

'Don't tease me, Luke.'

'I'll keep this to myself but know that we're watching.'

CHAPTER FIFTY

I wake feeling horrible. Between my weird dreams and the way my head is throbbing, I can't believe that it's still dark outside.

I have no idea what woke me and slowly look to see that I'm alone in the bed.

Not the room though.

A figure stands by the closed door.

I blink once.

Twice.

The figures dives towards me.

Opening my mouth to scream, a hand falls onto my face, covering most of it. The weight of my attacker pushes me into the hard mattress.

Kicking and bucking, my attempts to get out from under him is futile. I shout against the palm making it hard to breathe. It's getting harder and harder to draw enough air.

Wild eyed and frantically trying to get free, I go for the eyes. Nails out, I don't hold back and when my attacker makes a sound of pain, it fuels my fight reflex.

After everything that has happened, I won't be taken down like this.

'You bitch!'

That voice. I know it.

The slap comes from nowhere. I see stars and taste blood.

For a moment, I stop fighting.

'I knew it was you.' Captain Jorge's tone has me finally able to focus. 'I watched you all night dancing. Only someone of noble blood could dance as perfectly as you. I would've arrested you downstairs hours ago if it wasn't for the company you keep. The bounty on your head is huge. It will make my career. I have no idea how you survived that attack in the last tavern but when I looked for you, you were gone. All my men died. I feared you had too and that I wouldn't get my reward.'

Straddling me now, Captain Jorge wraps his calloused hands around my neck and squeezes. Cutting off my supply of air completely. It's impossible to cry for help.

'Dead or alive it said. And I'm going to enjoy killing you.' He's insane. A man possessed. His face is contorted. I know he will not let go until my heart stops beating.

Mouthing Zeke's name, over and over, I have no idea what the Captain did to him.

My attempts to get free are useless. His anger eats up the space, surrounding me with the promise of death.

Frantic eyes fixed on what he is doing, he doesn't care that I'm drawing blood as I rip his hands with my nails.

Then his focus falters for a second and he's no longer looking at his hands, but at my chest.

A flicker sparks in my mind and I realise I'm half nude with only my undergarments on. I don't remember how or why I'm naked. A blurry memory of me wanting to be comfortable flutters through my mind.

Darkness blurs the outside of my vision. My lungs scream.

A new wave of panic blooms when his eyes skim down my body. One of his hands loosens, allowing me to suck a hungry gasp of sweet air.

Thinking it's my chance to get away, I try to push at the single hand pressing me down into the mattress and receive another slap for my efforts.

Groaning, I cling to consciousness with every last bit of strength. Trying to scream when his hand brushes the skin above my breast, I punch him in the side four times and love when I hear him grunt.

I get another slap.

'What is this?' he says a little deranged.

Pulling the gold chain up, I realise what he means when the emerald flashes in the space between our bodies.

'Naughty, little bastard.' Jorge tsks. He's smiling like he's having the best time ever. 'Stealing from the Queen. Well, I could always say that I just found you naked. In the bed of some man you met on this filthy road. You whore!'

'Fuck you!' I manage through my crushed windpipe.

Jorge finds that hilarious. 'That's right. Fight me to the end. It's what your *husband* did and he is dead!'

No! 'What did you do?'

Jorge doesn't answer my question, his gaze sits hungry on the emerald and he practically licks his lips as he grips it and holds it carefully in his palm.

Thunder shakes the room. Lightning lights up the space, adding to the horror of this situation.

Jorge looks like a demon on top of me. One hand still wrapped around my neck, his body locks mine down completely.

'This could make me a rich man.'

I try to fight when he pulls the chain from my neck, manoeuvring both his hands so that the pressure on my throat is still there. There is no doubt in my mind that he has done this before. A murderer and a criminal wearing the crest of my family.

The absence of the stone is like losing a piece of my soul.

He grasps the emerald like it is the most beautiful thing he has ever held in his life. Something precious.

'A very, very rich man indeed. I will...' A wave of emotion passes over his face. His brow furrows until his face is set in a deep scowl.

The hand around my neck softens a little.

I can feel the tension in his muscles growing.

Silence descends and I can't look away as he whispers, 'what is going on?' to the stone in his palm like he is expecting it to answer.

I have no idea what is happening but deep in my gut I know something is about to.

There is a heartbeat of suspense.

One.

Two.

Then he throws his head back and screams a sound that has me freeze in terror. I clap my hands over my ears to drown out the sound. A booming wave of thunder swallows his noises as if the Gods are in on this.

Jorge's hand disappears and I suck in a jagged, painful breath and scramble away when he jumps off the bed, crying out.

Curled against the headboard, I watch in utter horror as he flings his hand back and forth. I might be mistaken but the emerald doesn't fall. It appears to be stuck to his skin.

'Get it off. Get it...' Frantic, he looks to me as if remembering that I'm here.

A horrible choking sound comes from his throat and he takes a single step towards the bed. My heart races watching the blood begin to spill from the sides of his mouth. He looks grey.

'You whore...you...'

Gurgling on what I can only assume is blood as it flies from his mouth, Jorge's eyes roll to the back of his head, showing me the whites.

He collapses in a heavy heap on the hard floor.

Silence.

Stunned, I sit, half naked, holding my neck. My ears ringing from the lack of noise.

What the fuck just happened?

CHAPTER FIFTY ONE

'Susi!' The door swings open, slamming into the wall. Zeke stands like the attractive god he is, in the doorframe, taking in the carnage. Every emotion flicks over his features. Shock. Rage. Concern. Confusion.

It's a complete contrast to my own. Terror. Relief. Loneliness.

'You're not dead?' I whisper. I've been sitting here for what feels like days, rocking back and forth, imagining the worst.

'Shit, Princess.' Zeke closes the door to our room, steps over the body like he couldn't care about all the blood and death and wraps me in his arms.

Oh Gods. 'He said he killed you.' My voice is a muffled groan against his shoulder.

'It would take more than a piece of shit like him to kill me. I promise. I'm sorry I wasn't here. I went for a walk when I couldn't sleep. What did he do? Are you hurt? Did he touch you?' Pulling me back, Zeke does a complete assessment of my body.

His fingers trace the forming bruises on my neck. 'I wish I could bring that fucker back to life so that I can kill him all over again.' The growl that comes from his chest does weird and wonderful things to my beaten-up soul.

Words don't come. *What do you say after what happened?*

'Did he...hurt you in any other way, Susi?'

Staring into his magnificent eyes, I shake my head, not wanting him to keep looking at me with that much worry. The thought of him being upset doesn't sit well. Zeke nods as if giving himself a moment to calm down. The energy surrounding him is volatile.

He searches my face and I honestly don't know what he sees.

Gripping my cheeks with his warm, strong hands, Zeke catches my gaze. 'You are safe. He can't hurt you again. You did well to defend yourself.'

I nod. That's all I can do.

Worry marks the space around his mouth. 'You're okay, Susi. I'm here.'

I nod.

I've never seen Zeke so upset. 'I shouldn't have left you. I keep leaving. Forgive me.'

Nodding, I hope he sees that I don't blame him. Why would I? This quest is mine alone. I wouldn't even be here today without him.

'Susi?'

I refocus to stare back at him.

'Breathe. In and Out.' It's a command that I follow. 'Good girl. And again. In and Out.'

For a few heartbeats that's all we do. Breathe in and out together.

I feel instantly better. Clearer.

Smiling warmly, Zeke tells me how good I'm doing. His praise eliminates the tension in my muscles. His closeness and general presence could also be doing that too.

'Now, speak to me, Princess.'

My mouth opens and closes a few times. He's so close. Our faces are only inches apart. 'I...he just died.'

'I know,' he replies calmly, like he understands exactly what happened in this room. 'He deserved everything he got. Now, we need to leave. I'm going to help you to get dressed and then we're going to get Horse and Toppin and we'll continue on our quest.'

Zeke is being nice and it's freaking me out even more. He laughs loudly when I tell him that.

'Fine. Get up and get dressed,' he says a little more Zeke-like. His hands are still holding my face though and I feel something sizzle between us. I'd give anything to feel his lips on mine. 'Come on.'

I follow his lead and get off the bed on shaking legs. My focus flicks to the dead body on the floor and then back up to Zeke when he tells me to look only at him. 'Good girl. Only look at me.'

Zeke doesn't make me feel awkward about being half naked. His focus is on my face as he holds out a fresh shirt and pants he must have taken from my bag.

Helping me to sit on the bed, he kneels before me and slips my feet into my boots once they are covered in thick socks.

Every time I accidently look toward Jorge, he reminds me to focus on him. 'Only me, Princess. You only look at me.'

Nodding, I stay locked in those ever-green depths, even when Zeke guides me to the door and we have to step over all the blood.

Faltering at the door, I touch my chest and then gasp. 'Zeke, he took my emerald.'

Zeke pats the pocket of his pants. 'I got it, Princess.'

Feeling a deep sense of relief, I get the hell out of the tavern.

CHAPTER FIFTY TWO

It's still dark out, maybe a few hours until dawn. Zeke is very attentive as he helps me onto Toppin and then secures my bag.

'What about Henry and the others?'

'They will understand. I'm sure once everyone wakes up to the dead body, it will be common knowledge.'

'Oh Gods. Zeke, we'll be wanted criminals!' This is a mess.

Zeke pulls himself up onto Horse and then studies me. 'Tell me now, Susyri. Tell me you want to continue on this quest to save your father or speak up if you want me to get you out of this kingdom, to safety and a new life. Just say the word and I will keep you safe. You do not have to do this anymore. You tried. Think of all you have been through. Is this quest worth your life?'

I'm completely taken off guard and touch my chest to find that the emerald isn't there. My fingers creep to my tender neck instead. *A new life out of this kingdom.* 'I can't,' I whisper. 'It's tempting, but I can't.'

Zeke glares. 'Why not? This is dangerous. You've been assaulted twice. Nearly eaten by Wolven and then the Xaver.

We are willingly going into the Dead Forest, Susyri. Why not?' he asks a little more forcibly. Toppin steps back and forth, impatient to start moving.

'It is my duty to my kingdom and my father, Zeke.'

He huffs a condescending sound and stares off into the distant trees. 'Duty. I hate that word.'

'I'm not much of a fan, however, it's my life. I didn't ask to be born into a privileged position. Yes, my life is hard being a bastard, but being on this road has shown me that I don't have it that bad. Look at Burk and Fi's life. Those children picking pockets on the streets. A messenger, as you say, came to me and told me how to save this kingdom from turmoil. My kingdom. Then, that is what I will do. It is not about me or my happiness or my own survival. If my father dies, there will be civil war. There are people who hate the Queen and will use me to get the throne. And there are people, like Captain Jorge, who will follow that horrible woman and the lives of all the people I have met on this road will be a hundred times worse.'

Closing my mouth when I feel it running away from me, I wait to see what Zeke will say. He is staring at me like I've just grown two heads.

'You speak of duty like someone I know,' he muses. 'My brother knew what it was to sacrifice for the better of others.'

Gods, I can feel his pain. 'He sounds like a remarkable man,' I offer.

Zeke nods. Horse seems just as impatient as Toppin to get moving.

'He was. It is I who continues to struggle with doing the noble thing.'

Mouth falling open, I realise that Zeke is not aware of how self-less and amazing he is. Henry hinted to it once and I didn't understand.

'Zeke, you saved my life on so many occasions. You met a girl on the road and sat in a tavern when, I know, I was being assessed by some questionable individuals. You stopped those men when they attacked me, without wanting anything in return. You threw yourself into a fight with mythical beasts, twice!' I emphasise, half shouting it.

'I saw you give coins to the children picking pockets when I walked away. I saw you take care of Henry and your friends when they were injured. I will never forget how you stayed behind to find Burk. I believe you understand duty, just fine. I don't know your story and I don't know what people you have to lead. Henry made a comment, but I don't *know*. All I know is that you're hurting and that's okay. But don't question yourself or your character. I am so happy to have met you, Zeke.'

It must be the multiple near-death experiences that have made me so talkative.

Zeke doesn't say anything. He just kicks his horse closer to mine until we are face to face. My poor heart flutters at the magnitude of him.

'I'm glad to have met you, Susyri.'

Leaning forward, I brace myself, unsure what he is going to do.

I have a few ideas of what I'd like it to be, but then he pulls something from his pocket and the emerald dangles between us.

It catches the moonlight and winks at me. Everything that happened in the room replays in my mind. It's weird to think that a piece of jewellery could kill someone—right? That's absurd.

Yet, when Zeke grabs at the stone with his palm, I jump to shout at him to drop it and then catch myself.

He doesn't seem at all bothered as he studies it and then reaches over and puts the chain back over my head. I bend to assist and sit up to find him running his hand over the green stone in thought.

'This is where it belongs.'

CHAPTER FIFTY THREE

The longer we go on the road, the thicker the forest gets. The darker the world becomes.

The energy is creepy. Much like my thoughts.

Frankly, they're a mess.

Zeke stops up ahead and I finally jump out of my head to realise that we have stopped at an intersection. Lucky Toppin was paying attention or I would have run into Horse.

'We're at the end,' Zeke announces.

'The end?'

It truly hits me. We're at the end of the Tilman Road.

The. End. Of. The. Road.

Shaking my head, I'm nervous all of a sudden. I didn't think I'd get here. Literally, I thought I would die, multiple times.

I kick Toppin to the middle. One way leads to more road and I swear the light seems brighter that way. The other is darkness and trees and vines and I swear, there is fog on the ground.

'You sure you don't want to go that way?' Zeke questions, pointing to the *safer* road. 'We could always disappear.'

Gods, it's tempting. 'You know, you can always—'

'I think we are long past me leaving you, Princess,' Zeke interrupts, shutting me up. It makes me smile.

'We got this far.'

'We can't take the horses.'

Zeke's words replay in my mind over and over as I stare up at him like a fool. 'Say that again,' I implore, for the second time.

'Come on Susi, you heard me. We can't take them any further.' He indicates towards what should be the rest of the road. Unfortunately, the gravel and dirt have disappeared under some seriously thick forest. Trees and branches and shrubs litter the space, blocking off any way for Horse and Toppin to move through it.

Gripping Toppin's reins, I eat my bottom lip trying to come to terms with what I know is the right thing to do. Leaving Toppin feels significant somehow. Like letting him go is severing the last of my connection with safety. From my life.

A mighty hand falls to my shoulder and I nod when Zeke tells me that it's time to keep moving.

He begins stripping both horses of their saddles, telling me that we can always replace the gear, like that is what has me all nervous.

It isn't. I don't give a shit about the tack. I care about what is going to happen to Toppin if I let him loose.

Our bags are thrown together on the damp ground and Zeke quickly ensures we have everything we need in the two carriers.

As if reading my mind, Zeke pulls Horse around so that he's facing the way we came. 'Go, boy. Go home.' He slaps him on the behind affectionately and the horse speeds away. He does the same to Toppin. 'Horse will look after your beast, Princess.' I don't trust myself to reply. 'Come, we have a great deal of distance to cover.'

Swallowing down the lump of emotion now sitting in my throat, I follow suit and pick up my now very heavier bag. Throwing it on my back, I take one last look behind me and to the small figures on the horizon.

'They'll be okay,' Zeke says as if understanding my trepidation. 'Horse will find his way home and take Toppin with him.'

'How can you be so sure?'

'Because they're smarter than humans,' he teases, or at least I think he is teasing. I can't actually tell with Zeke. 'Come.'

With my heart pounding against my chest, and with a heavy sigh, I steel my spine and walk into the Dead Forest.

CHAPTER FIFTY FOUR

'This place is far from dead,' I whisper, unsure why I feel the need to stay quiet. We haven't seen a single threat all afternoon.

'There's a number of reasons why it's called the Dead Forest. The bones of many stupid heroes lie buried under these leaves for one,' he states while stomping his booted feet for emphasis. 'But mostly, it's to keep stupid heroes away from Ekalus Peak.'

'So, it's all a lie? It's really not dangerous?' I muse, truly unsure what has me look over my shoulder for the hundredth time.

'No. It's deadly, Susi.'

Taking in my surroundings once more, I marvel at the sounds bombarding my senses. The insects and birds, the quick steps against the dead leaves in the distance, the shuffling movement of animals finding a safe place to hide when we approach.

'I don't see what all the fuss...Zeke!' Jolting forward as I see him stumble, I stop and bite my lip to keep from laughing at the sight of the large man now knee deep in what looks like muddy sand.

'What is this!' he demands, his face like living fire as he wiggles and grumbles to get free. 'I'm stuck.'

I lose the battle on my giggles. His glare could kill a man. 'Stop laughing and help!'

'Hold on,' I chuckle and Gods it feels good. Searching for something, I spy one of the thick vines wrapped around the closest tree and begin to cut a makeshift rope.

'Don't want to rush you or anything, but I am sinking.'

Swinging around from my task, my stomach drops at the sight of him now waist deep in the sand.

Cursing loudly, I start to cut like a mad person.

'Hurry up, Susyri!'

Heart pounding in my ears, I shout for him to hold on and finally get the vine off. Throwing it around a closer tree, I tie it off and rush back to the man now trying to keep his head above the quicksand.

'Zeke! Grab on.' Throwing the makeshift rope, I stand gaping for a moment as he tries to raise his hands. I can see the effort in the hard-set lines of his face. He's so weighted down that every move he makes just pulls him further under.

'Shit!'

Pulling back the rope, I don't think about what I'm doing and begin to tie the vine around my waist.

Blood pumping, I try to work as fast as I can with my hands shaking. It doesn't help when all I can hear is Zeke's muffled protest to stop what I'm doing.

'Don't you dare. Stay there, I'll be fine. Just give me...a...minute.'

'Shut up,' I call over my shoulder. This isn't helping me stay calm. My damn hands keep slipping from the knot and it takes me way too long to get it done. Testing that it is secure, I turn back around and assess the situation once more.

Zeke has sunk more and I feel sick about what I'm about to do.

'I said stay there, Susyri!' Gods he is bossy and arrogant and damn me but there is a small part of my soul that feels the need to listen.

Looking up from assessing the best route, my gaze collides with eyes so clear and stunning that I forget for a moment where I am. 'And I said, shut up,' I grumble. 'Okay, Susyri—' I say to pump myself up—'light steps. Go fast, but slow, and don't stop moving.' Speaking out loud seems to be helping, so I do it some more. I couldn't care less that Zeke is watching me.

'How can you go fast, but slow?' The damn male calls and I contemplate if I should just leave him to his fate.

'Do you want me to save you or not?' I bark out, bouncing on my feet, trying to gain the courage to do what I'm about to do. 'Right. I can do this. You got this, Susyri!' I pep myself and then step forward.

Moving into the quicksand, keeping my steps as light as possible, I hate the way the substance feels. It's like walking through syrup.

Focus locked with those breathtaking green eyes, I don't stop until I'm able to wrap my arms around Zeke's large form. The movements feel like they are in slow motion.

By the time I get there though, the sand is up to my chest.

'Okay.' I nod, mostly to try and reassure myself that I've done the right thing.

That I haven't just walked right into quicksand with a damn vine as a rope to try and pull a man out who weighs three times as much as me.

My mind is reeling, which is making it hard to formulate a better plan now that I'm mostly stuck in the sand as well.

'Now what?' I can hear the scepticism in his voice.

I move slightly and feel my body sink further down. 'I don't know.' I can barely breathe with the pressure. I think I'm really in trouble. 'I didn't think this far ahead. I just wanted to get to you,' I confess, feeling really silly.

Zeke frowns at whatever he sees on my face and I'm now the one receiving the glare, and it's a decent one. Damn arsehole. 'You have no idea what we do now, do you?'

'Well, I didn't see you coming up with a better solution,' I snap. He's infuriating.

I shuffle again. My arms are around his neck and I try to crush my body against his so that we are at least connected, which is impossible. The grains are like little razors, cutting and irritating my skin.

'My suggestion was for you to stay on dry land,' he retorts and my arms tighten around his body on instinct. I could strangle him. Being this close to Zeke is making the air thicker. He smells good, even after a day of travel and covered in muddy sand.

With my face next to his, I feel all self-conscious. Even in this dangerous situation, I feel the overwhelming need to place my lips on the side of his neck.

I can't shake the way it felt being in his arms last night when he carried me through the forest. The way he took care of me beside the river.

I'm losing my mind.

Lost in my own thoughts, I squeak a weird sound when Zeke's tree-trunk arms wrap around my middle. 'What are you doing?' I have no idea how he's able to move under the pressure. I can barely twitch my toes.

'Just hold tight.' He sighs in what I can only call exasperation.

'To what?'

'To me,' he barks and turns his head so that our faces are inches apart. Breathing in the same air, we stare, not doing or saying anything.

Confused and a little lightheaded, I stutter, 'I...I think we...'

I watch as a perfect smile fills his face. 'Just hold on. If you want to help, grab the vine too. This is going to be gruelling.'

Heaving, I suck in breath after breath. My chest, like the rest of my body, are burning.

Crawling along the hard ground, my legs slowly released from the sand, I collapse on my stomach with a groan.

Zeke is just as loud as he curses the world and falls down beside me.

The leaves littering the ground fly up at the impact of his heavy, muscled form.

I have no idea how long it took us to crawl our way out, but I don't think I can actually move anymore.

'My entire body is on fire,' I whine in a very un-lady-like way. Each word comes out strained and drawn out. 'That really sucked!'

'That's the biggest understatement I've heard.'

Glaring in his general direction, as I can't lift my head to make sure he can see me, I suggest, 'let's not do that again.'

'We need to keep moving. It's getting dark and it's going to get cold.'

My next groan is loud and drawn out.

CHAPTER FIFTY FIVE

'There's sand on my body in places sand should not be.'
Mumbling my anger to the heavens, I brush out my hair and glare at the clump of quicksand that falls on the ground beside me. I can't believe there is still sand on me. I've been cleaning myself for what feels like half the night.

Zeke gets the fire going and stands to admire his work, completely ignoring me. I did question if it was a good idea while we were out in the open like this and was out-ruled. Which doesn't seem fair seeing as there is only two of us.

I'm kinda grateful now for the heat. Well, more than kinda. I'm very grateful and shuffle a little closer to the flames. The temperature is dropping fast and we are surrounded by trees.

The clearing we chose isn't much. The ground is flat enough for him and I to sit side-by-side with the fire at our front. My view is the utter darkness of the thick forest. I'm just waiting for a set of glowing eyes to appear in front of me or something equally as terrifying.

I shiver at the bone-deep chill that ripples through my body. I'm starting to see why they call this place the Dead Forest. The moment the sun went down, the place seemed to come alive with activity. Mysterious howling and rustling fills the night, taking years off my life, I'm sure. I hear birds high above us and know that nothing friendly hunts during these hours. It doesn't help me to relax and rest after a gruelling day trudging through thick foliage.

Trying to braid the end of my hair, I cuss loudly and move my hands when Zeke tells me to. His replace mine in an instant. It's weird and intimate and I don't know what to do with my hands.

'Pass me the brush, you have a bit more sand here.' I can't decipher his tone and silently hand it over my shoulder. We sit in a comfortable silence while he fixes my hair. Once he's done, he ties it off and flings the braid over my shoulder.

'Thank you,' I murmur, very aware of our proximity.

His fingers brush against my neck and I close my eyes to the sensation. It feels good having him touch me after the experience of last night. 'I could kill him.'

'I think he's already dead.'

Then he does something that has my stomach back flip and do a little dance. Zeke brings his nose to the space between my shoulder and my neck and breathes in deeply. 'I want to kill him,' he says to my skin. 'For touching you. For hurting you.' Gods, his words settle against my soul and warm me from the inside out.

I'm bending my neck, giving him better access before I consciously realise what I'm doing.

I want to tell him that he's making it better by simply touching me. He chases away the pain and all my fears. But how does one say that without sounding like a fool?

'We should get some sleep. I'm afraid we will be up with the sun tomorrow.'

Nodding, I don't move and neither does he. As if he is waiting to see if I'll pull away, he finally moves both his legs to either side of my body and pulls me into his chest. I sit within his arms, feeling like anything could threaten me right now and I'd be safe.

Every inch of me is touching him and I melt into his chest. 'What monster do you think we will find guarding the road out of here?'

My head rests securely on his arm.

'Let's worry about one thing at a time. Sleep, Princess. I have you.'

And I do.

CHAPTER FIFTY SIX

My back hurts. My legs ache, and we seem to have been going in circles for the past three days.

The only thing keeping me sane is Zeke. The male who forges ahead, facing every bump in our path with a fierceness that seems to be growing.

With each passing day, Zeke changes. He appears to be made for this environment. His steps are featherlight. His ability to catch us dinner every night hints to a power and eye-sight that I can't even fathom and when I seek the comfort of his arms each night, he is warm against the cold. The dampness of the forest doesn't seem to affect him.

He almost seems to be having fun trudging through the wilderness.

I'm the complete opposite.

I trip and slide on the moss thick ground, while his steps are always confident. I get slapped and hit by every low-hanging branch possible, while he just brushes trees away like they're nothing but an annoyance to him.

I don't want to say anything but we aren't on any road anymore.

Zeke is incredibly tolerant with me. The only time he seemed to lose his patience is when we had to climb. I had a hard time finding the right rhythm to get up a sheer rock face safely. Zeke had to slow down a few times, and seeing me struggle, had to climb right under me with his hand on my butt, propelling me forward. There were moments were it felt like we were flying up the rock-face, he moved so fast.

Genuinely, I don't think it was me he was mad at for not being able to climb. I think it was the situation. I had a feeling that he knew a better way to get us to the top but for whatever reason, we couldn't do it.

Shivering, I try to contain my own body warmth by hugging myself.

We're high in the mountains somewhere, my sense of direction is so bad. The terrain is rocky and covered in thick, brownish grass mounds.

The trees no longer have leaves and are just stark-white trunks that look to have had their tops smashed off by something very big.

Zeke said two days ago that we're getting close to Ekalus Peak. I have no idea how he would know that. To me, the mountains still appears hundreds of miles away. I couldn't argue, he said it with such conviction.

The closer we get though, the more worried I become about the part of the quest that I still haven't found— 'the gift returned.'

As I trudge through the Dead Forest, I rack my brain to understand what that could be. The only thing I can come up with is the emerald.

Maybe that it was a gift to the Alpha Lord and he lost it, though why the 'messenger' would tell me to find the gift returned and then hand me the emerald is confusing. Perhaps it was just part of the riddle to get me to leave and stay on track.

Zeke pops his head from out of a cave opening he has been exploring for the last few moments. 'All is good, come. I smell rain.'

His eyes search the skies and I mimic the action with no clue what he means about smelling rain. He's done that a few times over the last few days. Stopping me to say that he smells or hears something that I can't. It's odd.

Night is falling heavily on the forest. The days are so much shorter here.

The cave is just a carved out burrow in the mountain. There's enough room for Zeke and I to spin around in a tight circle and that's about it. I'm safe standing to my full height though Zeke has to bend to accommodate his massive frame.

We quickly set up our bedrolls side-by-side at the back of the cave, with the stone wall as our headboard.

Zeke runs in and out of the space, collecting and sorting firewood. 'We will have to eat what's in our bags tonight.'

Nodding, I begin to rummage through our rationed food supply with a heavy heart. There isn't much left. A few pieces of bread and dried meats we purchased at the market. The fresh produce is long gone.

It doesn't matter. We will be mindful of what we consume.

Zeke sits heavily beside me once the small fire is lit. It's barely doing anything against the wind that now blows through the cave. However, it's warmer than being outside, and dryer.

The heavens have opened up and Zeke wasn't wrong, this storm is a big one. The rain hammers down instantly.

I rest my back on the cave wall and chew into the strap of meat. Zeke takes a piece and does the same while we watch the sheet of water blocking us from the forest.

'The mountain doesn't seem to be getting any closer,' I say through a mouthful of food. 'We've lost the road, haven't we?'

'No. At least I don't think so. There are other ways to get to the Peak. We will find one.'

CHAPTER FIFTY SEVEN

Teeth chattering, I toss and turn on my bedroll to find a warmer position.

It's futile.

The cave creates a tunnel for the freezing wind.

The rain is relentless.

The fire is long extinguished.

Zeke is close, trying to lend me his warmth. 'Susi, come here.'

I peek over and notice that he's moved against the back of the cave. Sitting up, he motions me over. I have no idea what he wants or what he has planned.

Every muscle in my body screams when I move. I'm stiff and frozen.

Crawling over to where Zeke is leaning up against the cave wall, I don't fight it when he helps me to straddle him. I'm not thinking about anything but warmth.

Sitting in his lap, Zeke pulls me against his chest. My front presses into his. My core hitting the bulge in his pants.

All thoughts of freezing to death disappear.

He doesn't seem at all fazed. Not like I am.

Tucking my legs around his body, he makes sure that I'm secure. My teeth hurt as they clack together.

Bringing his large hand to the back of my head, he silently pushes my head down until it's resting on his shoulder. His exquisite heat seeps into my body. My own personal flame. His scent surrounds me.

Sin.

'Thank you,' I whisper. Pressing my body closer involuntarily.

The tension between us increases with every heartbeat until he is all I think about. The overwhelming need to feel him on me, skin-to-skin, makes it impossible to think of anything else.

Something hardens against my core.

He wants me.

We've had moments like this before, however, this is proof that it's all not in my head.

Sitting up slowly, I find him staring and every part of me wishes that my clothes would disappear. That nothing was in the way of me feeling him. His ever-green eyes are piercing. Brighter in the darkness.

'Susyri, I don't want to do anything that you don't feel comfortable with. But I'd really like to kiss you right now. If you'd let me.'

My Gods. No one has even asked me if I wanted to be kissed before. Most men I've interacted with leak cockiness, and the handful of partners I've been with, have led our time together. As if taking control was somehow an attractive quality, and maybe I thought it was. I guess I never experienced *this* before. If I had, none of those boys would've had a chance, because I now know what a man is.

What real strength and power is. Zeke doesn't have to take what he wants. All he has to do is ask and I'd give him anything.

We've only really just met, and yet he has embedded himself so far under my skin that I'm afraid I won't be able to breathe without him. The fact that we are nearly at the end of our journey makes it harder to process. There is so much we don't know about each other.

I'm practically betrothed, for heaven's sake. Well, at least I was told I am.

My head is spinning right now.

How could I say no to this? I have wanted this for so long. Being against him. Feeling his desire. Nothing else seems to matter. Nothing. We could die tomorrow. We could freeze to death overnight.

'Yes,' I whisper.

Zeke makes one of his funny noises that vibrates against my chest and then his mouth claims mine.

My entire world shifts on its axis.

I gasp at the sensation that shoots down my spine, the emerald heats until it is almost painful. Zeke takes that opportunity to invade my mouth with his tongue and I'm lost.

Zeke kisses me like he does everything else in life, with a confident arrogance. I thought I'd been kissed before— I was wrong.

This is a kiss.

Reluctantly, I break it to breathe.

Sitting, I stare, my chest heaving. He does the same.

'We should sleep,' he states. His eyes are brilliant. His hand runs over my cheek and through my hair. I lean into the touch.

'Yeah, we should.'

Zeke studies my face. 'In a moment,' he growls each word and then he pulls my mouth back to his.

Moaning into his lips, I give in to his assault.

His desire presses against my centre.

Grinding and locked together, we fight the coldness of the night with the press of our bodies.

Fully clothed, both of us knowing this is all we will get tonight before our journey continues tomorrow.

CHAPTER FIFTY EIGHT

It's still raining when I wake the next day. The heat in the air is making it hard to breathe.

The tension and awkwardness between Zeke and I since I woke up, still wrapped around him, is thick and weird. He doesn't look happy as he stabs at the fire like it has offended him somehow.

'It's okay Zeke,' I say softly. I'm sitting at the entrance of the cave, watching the rain fall. It's not as heavy anymore and the sun is still out. It's kind of beautiful. The forest blanketed in mist has it not looking so frightening for a moment.

'What is okay?' he asks eventually. Gods, he is in a mood.

'If you don't want what happened between us to happen again. I understand. We were cold. It was the situation and this place. I don't hold you to anything if you regret what we did.' *Why does each word hurt to say?* Maybe because I don't want him to regret it. That my feelings for Zeke are growing.

'Susi, look at me,' he states in that bossy tone.

I comply for reasons that elude me. Our gazes lock and I didn't realise how sad I am until I find myself getting lost in those ever-green depths.

'I don't regret a thing,' Zeke says and while I believe him, I look away. He appears before me in a heartbeat, blocking my view of the forest.

I have to crane my neck back to stare up at him and what I see has me swallow the ball of sorrow that was threatening to choke me.

We just stare.

I watch as the expression on his face loses its hardness.

Sighing heavily, as if the weight of the world is on his shoulders, Zeke offers me his hand. 'Come, Princess.'

I take it instantly, my body moving on its own. Zeke pulls me to my feet and leads me out into the rain.

I gasp the moment we step out of the cave. I'm instantly drenched. 'Zeke?'

'Just come.' He smiles and it's the most beautiful sight in the world. Pulling me into his chest, Zeke wraps an arm around my middle and takes my right hand in his.

My entire body freezes as slowly and confidently, Zeke and I begin to dance.

My heart is pounding.

Staring, wide eyed up at the man holding me, I fight the urge to weep at what we are doing. Water gets into my mouth, my eyes and drips down my back, but I don't care. 'What...what are we...'

Zeke holds me in his powerful gaze, his arms caging me securely against his body. 'We are dancing, Princess. I promised you that we'd dance in the rain.'

The world stills. I don't know what to say or do. My tears mingle with the water running down my face and after the initial shock wears off I sniffle and rest my head on Zeke's broad, hard chest.

I'm dancing in the rain.

'Thank you,' I whisper. Unsure if he can hear me, I lift my head to make sure and catch the pained expression on his face. I know that he is battling his own emotions. Even if I don't understand what is wrong, I know it's hurting him.

For a moment, I think he's going to kiss me but he spins me. I laugh at the sudden, swift and perfect movement. I'm dancing with Zeke, and Gods, he *can* dance. He moves with a grace and power that I'm becoming accustomed to.

Laughing, we both get absolutely saturated and neither of us care.

It's the most fun I've ever had in my entire life and I realise that I may be falling in love with the male with ever-green eyes.

CHAPTER FIFTY NINE

Back slamming against the trunk of a tree so big we can't see it's canopy, I groan in pleasure.

Gripping Zeke's travel cape, frantically trying to pull him closer, I match every move his mouth makes.

Tongues dancing, we devour each other, unfazed that we are out in the open.

Who is going to see us, the little forest creatures running around?

I haven't seen a single living creature in two days. It's just been walking and fighting against the overgrown foliage. The only thing I have to focus on is the incredible tension between us and the moments where we give in. However, it never goes beyond what we are doing now, even though I've tried multiple times to indicate that I'm ready and willing to go further.

Zeke was the one to start this session. I let him do whatever he wants while one of his hands holds me up by my butt and the other protects my back from the rough bark I'm crushed against.

My legs are wrapped around his middle and I feel everything. And I mean...everything.

His hardness fuels my desire and I grab at his shirt with the intent of pulling it off him and then find myself on wobbly legs, alone.

Zeke rubs at his face as he paces a few feet away, cursing the skies like they're the reason he won't take this any further.

Gripping the tree, I try to remember how to breathe properly after being kissed so completely. He does this a lot.

'Zeke, I told you that I'm not some precious woman who needs you to take it slow. If you don't want me, then just say so, because your messages are all weird.'

Zeke throws me a very 'don't be dumb' kind of look. 'Of course I want you. Gods above, look at me.' I take my fill of that impressive body and the very obvious desire in his pants. I practically lick my lips. 'Fuck me, Susyri. Please don't do that!'

'Do what?' I manage to get out and even I hear the desire in my voice. What I would give to just...

'That!' He gestures towards my general direction.

'What is the problem?'

He stops pacing and we end up staring from either side of the small clearing. 'There are things about me that you don't know. Things that we need to discuss before we take this step.'

'Okayyyy. Well, what kind of things?' He goes back to pacing and it's making me uncomfortable. Shit. 'Are you married?'

Again, I get the 'don't be dumb' look.

'It was a legitimate question,' I snap. Now eating my bottom lip, guilt blooms in my gut. I haven't shared everything with him either. 'Well, I guess now is the time to let you know that I might be betrothed,' I venture, watching his every move.

Zeke stops and looks over at me sharply, those green eyes narrowed in my direction. 'I didn't agree or sign anything and my father hasn't approved it either. It was just something that happened before I left on this quest.'

Why is my heart pounding so hard?

'Susyri, I don't give a shit about some human custom or a man who thinks he has some claim to you. If you didn't accept an engagement or promise yourself to anyone, it means nothing to me.' Zeke shakes his head and scrubs at his face.

That was a weird response, and yet, I feel so light that I don't think anything he can say right now could make me not want him.

It's then I realise how much of a burden keeping this to myself was. 'Then what is it?'

Back and forth he goes. He's making my head spin.

'Zeke! Stop moving and just tell me. Whatever it is, it doesn't matter because I think I might be...in love with you.'

Mouth clamping shut, I have no idea why I said what I just said or that I was even thinking this. It just came out and I wish like anything to be able to scoop up the words and place them back in my throat.

We stand, staring for too long and the tension between us turns awkward. He doesn't feel the same, that much is true, because he just hangs his head.

Oh my Gods. Why did I say that? I've ruined everything.

My face heats.

'Susyri...I,' but before Zeke can finish his sentence the heavens open. The blanket of rain that falls is instant and saturating and I follow when Zeke tells me to run. We have been out here long enough to know that this kind of rain in the Dead Forest is dangerous.

'I'm not hungry. I might just try and sleep. Could you wake me for my turn for watch?' I ask the silent man eating on the other side of the small fire we made. We eventually found another little burrow big enough for us to rest out of the storm.

We haven't spoken a single word to each other since finding it. I'm mortified at what I said earlier and am embarrassed to have made a fool of myself. I told Zeke that I love him...what the fuck?

I don't even know if I do. Well, I think I might.

I do.

I think I've been falling for him since the first moment I saved him on the road. It turned from attraction to a feeling of safety and reassurance quickly. Seeing him after that, in the taverns and the markets, all those times, his face gave me a sense of security and calm when I was truly alone on this quest.

I think I loved him before he saved me, over and over.

Now, I have ruined our friendship and it is eating me up.

Zeke just nods in acknowledgement of my words and I sigh and find my bed roll.

Sleep won't come easily. Not when I'm beating myself up for my behaviour.

CHAPTER SIXTY

'Is that...a...a dragon?'

Breathing is difficult as I look once more over the boulder. The gigantic, winged beast slumbers peacefully beside a crystal lake.

I actually fear that it will be able to hear my raging heartbeat.

Trying to be quiet, I look towards the well-manicured path he sleeps across.

The road out of here.

The fact that Zeke looks mildly unsettled does not help my panic as he quietly crouches beside me. We have barely spoken all day. We woke up with the sun, packed our camp and just kept moving.

My fight or flight reflexes are in turmoil right now.

I have to sit.

Leaning on the rock for support, I try to remember to not panic.

'You know, I could live the rest of my life never seeing a mythical being every again.'

Wolven. Xaver. Now dragons!

'Well, I think we found our monster guard,' Zeke announces, still gazing over the boulder. Looking at me with those ever-green eyes, his brow furrows at whatever he sees on my face. 'Susi, I think we need to find a different way to the Peak. Dragons are not beings you want to mess around with.'

'I don't think I have a choice. It's what the messenger said.'

Shit. This is it. I made it to the end of the Tilman Road and now I'm at the end of the Dead Forest. I've just got to get past…that.

Gripping the stone that I no longer worry is hidden away, I try to work through the emotions rolling through my mind.

'Well, we got this far. I can't go back now.' Forcing my legs to stand, I take some deep, steadying breaths. 'I have to get past the monster and then I will be granted an audience with the Alpha Lord. The thing looks asleep, so I'll just sneak past. You can come or stay, it is your choice. I won't risk you. If this is where our journey together ends, then I am forever grateful.'

Not waiting for him to respond, I quietly move from out of our hideout. I know I'm not being fair to him. I just can't help it. I'm embarrassed and a little heartbroken and rejected.

The breath coming from the sleeping monster consumes the world. The noise almost deafening.

Zeke is whisper-shouting for me to come back.

Waving my hand in his general direction to keep quiet, I try to work out my route with each step. The path directly below the dragon is covered but if I can walk around the lake and maybe meet up with the road behind the beast…

Praying, I move, very aware that Zeke is not following. Sweat beading on my forehead, I try not to look at the monster. Every noise I make causes my blood to pump harder.

I make it halfway around the dark body of water and begin to believe my plan may work when a terrifying chuckle fills the forest.

The trees shaking under the vibrations.

A small noise escapes my lips as I slowly turn and see eyes like night looking back at me. The monster lifts his head and I get a full glimpse of the beauty of the creature. Its red and orange scales glisten in the sunlight as it stretches its lizard-like body; its leathery wings touching the tops of the forest canopy with the movement.

'What have we here?' it asks and I have to cover my ears at the intensity of its tone. *It can fucking speak!* 'A snack.'

There are no words to describe my terror.

I want to run and hide. Gods, I am so sick of these roadblocks. I just want this to be done. I steel my spine. The road is just there, within reach. The messenger said I just have to get past this monster and then I'll get my audience with the Alpha Lord.

Taking a few deep breaths, I muster up every ounce of courage I have. 'I need to get to Ekalus Peak.'

Laughing, the dragon drops his head over the lake, his yellow teeth pulled back in a grin. 'No one gets past me, human.'

I watch it pull back and take a breath. 'Oh shit!'

Smoke billows from its gigantic mouth just before fire erupts. Filling the forest with heat and colour.

I run back towards the boulder just as its head moves in my direction. Fire devouring everything in its path.

I don't stop moving but my useless human legs aren't fast enough.

Heat scorches my hair and then I'm falling.

The ground rushes to meet me and I trip and fall in a heap on the hard ground.

Pain erupts along every inch of my body.

Pushing it all away, I spin and scream at the sight of the smiling dragon, its black eyes focused on me as it laughs.

It draws back its neck like it did before and...Covering my head, I wait for death.

CHAPTER SIXTY ONE

It takes my mind a ridiculous amount of time to register that I'm not being burnt alive despite the unbearable heat I can feel.

Slowly lowering the arms covering my head, I notice the wall of flame bending around me first.

Confused, I finally look up.

My shout of despair is gobbled by the sound of rushing fire as I see Zeke standing protectively over me, arms stretched, taking the full force of the dragon's breath.

But...

What is blocking the fire is not his back but his...wings. Massive, bird-like wings fill my vision. Their colour a perfect brown, with lines of dark mahogany running through the feathers.

Time slows down.

My gaze travels over every feather. His back is bent, his face scrunched in determination as if the weight of the flames is hard to bear.

My first thought is—is the fire hurting him?

The fire dies as quickly as it came. Zeke's ever-green eyes flash to me briefly and for a moment I see the flicker of deep sorrow. Then he turns and stands to his full height, his wings outstretched, keeping me hidden.

It's a sight to behold. The wingspan is unfathomable. Where they are attached to his back is full of shorter, light brown feathers and they're now scattered all the way down his spine. Not a hint of fire damage mars his perfect skin...feathers...wings...whatever I'm looking at.

The ground shakes under the laughter of the dragon. 'Oh, it has been an age since I have seen one of your kind, Ekalus Warrior. I heard you were lost, boy. That your grief drove you from your destiny. And here you are, protecting a human.' The same otherworldly laughter shakes the trees.

'What?' I whisper, not able to form a complete thought. I hurry to my feet. Zeke frowns over his shoulder. His face is covered in emotion.

Sadness. Regret. Anger.

'Ezekiel, your father would not be pleased. Look at how hurt the human is, there are too many emotions there, boy. I hope you know what you are doing.'

Ezekiel?

Flashes of a dream race through my mind.

'Your father?' My voice is barely audible. 'Who is your father?'

'Never mind, you will both die,' the dragon declares, reminding me that we are still in terrible danger.

'Susi!' Swinging around supernaturally fast, Zeke grabs me around the middle before I can register what is happening. The world passes by in a blur as he flies me, at speed, through the thick forest.

The moment we stop, I push out of Zeke's hold.

Stumbling, I fall on my hands and knees and expel the limited contents in my stomach.

'Susi...'

I swing around to the stunning man, and the wings that fill my vision.

They are magnificent. He is...an Ekalus *Warrior*.

'Don't!' I cut him off, trying desperately to get air into my constricted lungs. Hating being on the ground in such a vulnerable position, I scramble to my feet and wipe my mouth with the back of my hand.

Tears fall freely down my face and I realise that they're not from fear of being face-to-face with an Ekalus, but his betrayal. 'You are an Ekalus!' I shout, not caring that he looks just as messed up as I feel.

'I wanted to tell you.'

Covering my ears at the purity and mesmerising sound of his voice, I realise that he was probably putting some kind of cover over his otherworldly-ness this entire time. Even his ever-green eyes are greener. Sharper. There is also a curve to them now that wasn't there before, like he isn't trying to hide the beast under his skin anymore.

His face falls at the sight of my tears and I take a shaking step back when he reaches out as if to touch me.

'Who is your father?' I manage. My heart pounds so hard in my chest that it hurts. It hurts. This really, really hurts.

I loved him. I trusted him.

Pained, Ezekiel seems lost and I don't care that it breaks my heart further seeing him so upset. A stupid part of me wants to step forward and throw my arms around him and make sure that he's okay.

'Who is he!' I bellow, knowing deep in my soul that I know the answer and that it's going to break me when I find out.

Zeke, *Ezekiel*, stands tall, his face hardening before he says, 'my father is the Alpha Lord Michael, the leader of the Ekalus.'

Sobbing now, I grip my chest. The jewel smacks into my hand and for the first time, it's not hot. It's icy cold. 'You are his son? After everything we have been through, the danger, the pain that I lived with knowing my father will die if I fail. All this time, you could've helped me. You could have taken me to him!'

'I have—'

'No. *Ezekiel*. I see what I am now, I was just the entertainment. The fool that made you laugh for a split moment in your eternity. What was I? The stupid human girl you picked up on the road to play games with. Is this some kind of Ekalus monster game your race plays before you eat one of us?' I'm yelling, each word spills from my lips. Each word spits with hatred.

Of all the monsters I have faced, the irony is the one saving me was the one I needed to be afraid of the most. Pieces of the puzzle that is Zeke start falling into place.

The Wolven. The Xaver. The way he saved me over and over. The dream, that I was stupid enough to have thought was my imagination, when really it was an Ekalus outside that tavern window.

Turning, I fall to the ground, my heart breaking as I realise what I was beginning to feel for this man…this being. For the first time in my life, I felt safe and secure. I was myself. I was happy. All that has been ripped out from under me.

He is an Ekalus.

'You were never any of those things, Susyri. I would never—'

'Please,' I cut him off. I just can't bear any more. I want to weep and release this pain before it kills me. 'Go,' I whisper. 'Please, leave me alone.' He knew my story and didn't care. He could have prevented all of this. The attacks. The death.

'Susi.'

'Please,' I cry.

The wind that is caused when Ezekiel lifts off the ground pushes me further into myself.

Alone, I let my grief consume me.

CHAPTER SIXTY TWO

Stumbling through the forest and eventually find the burrow we stayed in last night.

Head pounding from crying, I end up crawling into the cave and curling in on myself. I have no idea how I still have tears to shed. They just keep coming.

How could this have happened? How could I fall in love with an Ekalus? I have been raised to think of them as monsters. Killers who love to terrorise humans. Stories and tales paint them as men and women who appear like humans and can shift into mighty birds of prey. Yet, every story tells us that they are obviously different when in their human form. Tall like ogres. Sharp teeth and nails. It is what gives us comfort.

It's all horse-shit.

Ezekiel is just like any other man. He walks like one, talks like one, and he's arrogant like every other one I've interacted with.

The eyes are strange and his body is cut like nothing I've ever seen. Also his features look fake, they are perfect.

No fangs or claws though, and I should know, I've kissed that mouth and felt those hands caress my skin in affection.

Definitely no signs of the monster.

Gods, I don't know if I cry harder at the fact that he had me fall in love with him or if I hate myself for how I reacted to finding out who he truly is. Or maybe it's both.

I've given up everything.

I've been through so much.

Rolling onto my back, I let the last of the tears fall as I study the cave ceiling. I can't do this. I'm a failure. I can never get past the dragon.

'You're not a failure.'

Squealling, I jump to my feet and ready myself for battle and come face-to-face with the beautiful woman from the garden. She appears just like I remember her. Long white-blonde hair to her hips. The same silver gown that sways on a breeze I don't feel.

'You...you're a messenger.' What Zeke said bounces around in my head. Everything he said does. I start to build a bigger picture of what has happened over the last few weeks.

I have no idea if I'm in danger or not.

She appears to be alone. This breathtaking lady is just standing in the cave in the middle of the Dead Forest. And I know I didn't say that thought about being a failure out loud. 'How did you...Where did you come from?'

Her silver dress billows around her as she steps forward, each move utterly graceful. I take an involuntary step back.

'I go where I am needed.'

'I don't need anything. What I need is to be left alone.' I can't take much more of these beings.

At my breaking point, I couldn't care if she rips my spine out of my mouth or eats me alive, or whatever messengers do. I'm tired.

Sitting back down, I find a stick to play with.

'We don't eat people,' she says, clearly disgusted by my thoughts.

'Why did you send me on this quest? I was never going to survive.' Furious, I begin to dig a hole in the hopes of maybe making it big enough to bury myself in for a while.

'I think you'd need a bigger stick for that,' the messenger states. Looking up sharply from my task, I eye the beautiful woman who messed up my life.

'I truly thought I could save my father.'

'And you can. All is not lost Susyri. A road isn't just made of gravel and dirt. There are many paths to the Peak.'

Zeke said the same thing.

Now I'm thinking of him again. Damn her and her meddling.

'Of course all is lost. I can't get past the dragon. I nearly died. I would have if it wasn't for...for...' Gods, I can't even say his name. 'I have no idea where the gift is for me to return it, and it's useless,' I shout.

Holding me in her silver eyes, the messenger nods solemnly. 'All heroes face a moment along the journey where all seems lost, Princess Susyri.'

'I am no hero. I'm nobody. A bastard princess.'

The messenger glides over to where I sit and folds herself gracefully on the ground beside me. I'm in too much of a mood to register that she is so close. She smells like vanilla and honey.

My tears have started again.

'A hero doesn't have to be the strongest warrior or the greatest knight. They don't need to have won battles and killed for victory. A hero just needs bravery and duty. They need heart and kindness. A hero, Princess Susyri, is someone who can fight through the struggles life throws and can still love enough to sacrifice themselves for others. This quest is yours and yours alone because you are those things. It is up to you if you embrace that and live out your destiny.'

Sniffling, I wipe at my face.

'I think you know why your love kept his secrets. You have all the answers, Susyri. You just have to remember.'

Turning toward her with the intent of asking her more questions, I find myself completely alone with my memories of a dream replaying in my mind.

CHAPTER SIXTY THREE

Determined not to vomit again or think too hard on how miserable it is travelling without Zeke, I study the dragon and the path I must take.

Going home is not an option. I will be damned if I fail now.

It has taken me way too long to find the lake again without Zeke's help and night has settled heavily on the Dead Forest.

Using the cover of darkness, I sit on the boulder I hid behind yesterday and try to come up with a different tactic. Options go through my mind, each one seeming destined to fail as I push them away. I've learnt so much on this journey. I've learnt so much from Zeke that I know I need to take my time to work this puzzle out. I know I can work this out. Zeke and the messenger told me that there are many paths to the Peak.

Yesterday I tried to be sneaky and go through the forest around the beast.

What if I didn't do that? What if I get close to it, get back on the road it's guarding and hope he doesn't hear me? The dragon won't be expecting that.

Last time, I was trudging through the foliage like an ogre in one of the castle stories.

It takes me a little longer than I'd like to find the courage to move. Reminding myself that I have faced attack after attack and survived, that I am stronger than I think, I eventually push off the boulder, determined to finish this quest.

Feet light, I run on tip toes, my heart hurting as it pounds within my chest.

Trying to stay quiet, I slowly move closer to the sleeping monster. It's scales shine in the moonlight and it's just as frightening up close as it was from afar yesterday.

All that's going around in my mind is that it can breathe fire and that I'm going to be scorched alive.

Thankfully, the rise and fall of his chest is the only movement it makes.

Sneaking around the tail, I hold my breath when it moves lazily from side to side.

Muscles tense, I eventually get around the mighty form and with a glimmer of hope, turn my back and creep along the road it was guarding.

I think I did it! I think I'm actually going to get to Ekalus Peak…maybe I am capable of—

I squeal when the world begins to shake.

I don't bother looking over my shoulder, I drop the bag on my back and run.

Suddenly, I'm lifted off my feet when something painful slams against my side.

Flying through the air, I land at the edge of the lake, gasping for breath. *It whacked me with its tail!*

'Tsk. Tsk. Tsk. Little human girl. You aren't that good at playing mouse. For your efforts, I will kill you quickly.'

Shit. Forcing myself onto hands and knees, I try to scramble away. To find cover in the boulders to my right.

Any moment now I will feel that fire.

The dragon roars a sound that has two trees to my left fall to the ground with a mighty bang and I turn to look over my shoulder and stop moving.

Ears ringing, I manage to sit up, my eyes adjusting eventually to what I'm seeing.

'Zeke!' I shout, a different kind of terror turns my blood to ice watching the Ekalus land on the dragons back, driving his sword through the scaly hide. His wings outstretched.

The dragon bellows a noise that has my insides turn to liquid.

Dodging each one of the dragon's blows, Zeke battles the beast, his voice cutting through my fear, 'run, Susi!'

Finding my feet, I sprint towards the path to Ekalus Peak. Legs pumping, I come to a screeching halt when I hear the dragon's triumphant laughter.

The world stills as I twist around to see Zeke, wings distorted, in the crushing grip of the beasts claw.

Two things happen in that moment that will change me forever.

My eyes lock with those ever-green eyes and Zeke mouths, 'run,' just as the dragon squeezes. The sound of cracking bones stops my heart. I scream watching Zeke's lifeless body fly through the air, thrown into the lake with a deadly slap.

'No! Zeke!'

Uncaring of the ball of fire that shoots towards me, I run and dive in bitterly cold water, the heat of the dragon's breath burning my legs before I'm fully submerged under.

Zeke is a dull light within the darkness of the lake and I will my body to move, to get to him. With each stroke into the ancient liquid, I begin to lose my orientation.

Ignoring the way my chest scream for air, I finally wrap my arms around the sinking male's middle. But up has no meaning in the dark.

I fight the growing need to draw in air.

I can't give up. Not now. Zeke came back for me. I'm so mad at him and so in love with him at the same time, it hurts to think that I've lost him forever. That the world has lost this magnificent male forever.

Desperate, I don't question where the light that appears from my neck comes from or the way it points to a hole in the wall of the lake to our left. The small bubbles popping out of it could only meaning one thing. Air.

With the last of my dying strength, I drag the dead weight towards our only hope for survival.

As we approach the opening, both Zeke and I are sucked into a whirlpool.

Wrapping my arms and legs around the Ekalus, I bury my head into his chest, afraid to be separated while the world turns black.

CHAPTER SIXTY FOUR

I finally died.

After everything that has happened, Death has finally caught up with me. I know this because when I open my eyes all I see is brown. The world is devoid of any other colour.

The ground below me is soft and feathery, another indication that I'm no longer in the living world.

It is mighty comfortable though and if I am dead, it means my quest is over and I can finally sleep.

I curl into the solid warmth beside me, I'm ready to nap for a few weeks.

Something muffled distracts me. It's getting louder and louder before all I can hear is yelling and shouting. Not a great afterlife I've found myself in. And why am I wet?

Wait.

Why *am* I wet?

Zeke.

I raise a hand to touch the perfect sheet of bird-like feathers and finally turn my head. My heart flutters and stops at the sight of ever-green eyes staring at me.

'How are you alive? I heard your body break!' I frantically run my hands over his body. He is okay.

'The magic of these mountains are healing. You saved me, again. Getting me here like you did, saved me.' The breathtaking male smiles and I find myself mimicking the action.

'I thought you said I didn't save you last time.' I'm distracted by the cocoon his wings have us locked in.

Zeke chuckles. 'You saved me the moment I met you on that road, Susyri. I was just too lost in my own grief and guilt to see it at first. You see,

I was on this road, lost to my sorrow for years. Lost and unwilling to accept the reality that I'm the future Alpha Lord. Something my brother should've been. A brother I loved and lost. And then I met this human girl with gorgeous black hair and a face no painter could ever match in beauty.'

Oh Gods, I'm blushing.

'She was brave and courageous and kind. And she showed me that duty is something to embrace and live with. To make your own. I have watched you give up everything for your kingdom and it placed a mirror to my own choices.'

'Zeke, I—'

He stops me with a gentle caress of his finger against my lips. 'I regret so much in my life. Hurting you is my greatest disappointment.

You put me back on my true path and I will be forever grateful to you. You have done me a great service, Susyri.'

'Zeke. I didn't do anything.' Cupping his face, I hope he can see how genuine I am when I apologise. 'I let my prejudice get in the way of my heart. I was so scared and lost. But I remember that night in the tavern, when you were talking to that male, Luke.'

Zeke seems shocked. 'I thought you were asleep. You were incredibly drunk.'

Conceding, I tell him I was barely conscious. 'You said that going home meant you could never leave. That your father said it would be you accepting your duty as his successor. Zeke, I don't blame you for not taking me straight to Ekalus Peak. I don't want to change your future or force you to do something you don't want to just for my own quest. I can go the rest of the way on my own.'

He gives me a funny look before he says, 'actually Princess,' and then unfolds his wings.

I have to blink at the onslaught of light. With his wings no longer blocking the world, I am met with a picturesque starry sky and the faces of otherworldly beings staring, open-mouthed at us.

'Zeke, where are we?' I whisper, afraid to move.

Zeke chuckles. 'Ekalus Peak, Princess Susyri. You did it. Welcome to my home.'

CHAPTER SIXTY FIVE

I don't know who is helping who when we both sit up. We both groan and I'm guessing his body is hurting just as much as mine is. My leg is throbbing.

The large, decorated garden we have fallen smack in the middle of seems to be hosting a feast of some kind.

Out of the crowd comes a shouting Ekalus beauty. She falls beside Zeke and I feel a sting of emotion I have never felt before watching him embrace the red headed goddess.

I actually pat at my hair knowing it's a mess. My water clogged clothes stick to my very human form and I catch Zeke's little smirk.

Throwing him a very impressive glare, his laughter sets everyone in motion.

Wrapping an arm around my middle, I stand awkwardly beside him. 'Mother, I am perfectly fine.'

Holy damn!

It's Zeke's mother.

She rises along with us, her eyes narrowed at her son.

Gods, she is intimidating and beautiful. Tall and lean, with wings of pure white. She doesn't seem too impressed by what Zeke has just said. 'Perfectly fine!' she practically shouts, the sound like bells twinkling in a breeze. 'You have been gone for countless moons, Ezekiel. Do you know how much your father and I have worried. How much your flock has worried!'

She indicates to the horde of Ekalus watching Zeke get chewed out by his mother. On and on she goes about how inconsiderate my companion has been, how selfish. She ends with how much she has missed him.

It's clear that she is hurt by his actions and if what she is reprimanding him for is true, I don't blame her. He deserves it.

Observing the crowd though has me shuffle on my feet and step closer to the big male who has appeared to have forgotten that I'm here. Super conscious of his wings, I try to make myself as small as possible. There are men and women everywhere. All winged. All wearing clothes that hug their bodies.

The males are big shouldered and scary looking. The muscles on them are impressive and very, very frightening. I spy numerous weapons on most of them. Rounded, curved eyes of every colour track my movements. The women are breathtaking.

I scan for any sharp teeth and claws and come up with nothing.

Until a shriek from up above has me flinch and practically throw myself into Zeke's side. His wings snap out and curl around me, locking me safety in their embrace.

Feeling protected, I stare wide eyed and gape in awe as a beast flies overhead.

A beast so grand in size that the dragon we just faced looked like a baby monster. It's mighty black wings flap as it soars away and I'm left processing that I just saw a fully shifted Ekalus for the first time.

'Ezekiel.' It is the power in the voice that draws my focus from searching the sky for more predators. The male who steps through the throng of the crowd is terrifying. He is stunning in a brutal looking way. It makes me want to run back and battle the dragon again.

I know who he is without an introduction. He is the Alpha Lord Michael. Zeke's father. They look alike. The same dark hair and sharp features. Tall. Strong. Intimidating.

'Father,' Zeke replies formally. 'I have returned,' he declares like it is some kind of amazing revelation and I frown at the whispering voices that fill the garden.

The Alpha Lord stands before his son, his thick arms wrapped across his chest. 'You know what I said about what it means when you return, Ezekiel.'

Regret hits me hard as the realisation of what Zeke has given up for me sinks heavily in my soul.

'I do.'

The pair stare. And stare, and stare, until the Alpha Lord does something that shocks me. He steps forward and pulls Zeke into a hug.

A hug.

This powerful, winged man who can turn into a monstrous bird-beast is hugging his son. I have never been hugged by my father. A king doesn't hug...right?

'Welcome home, my son.'

'I'm sorry, Father.' Zeke is whispering into the Alpha Lord's shoulder and I only hear his apology because Zeke's wings are still holding me close to his body.

There is a lot of back slapping between the pair. Zeke's mother wipes at her eyes and the Ekalus watching are doing so now with wide smiles on their faces. It's all so...welcoming.

'And what had you change your mind and find your way home?'

Before I can fully understand what the Alpha Lord has just asked, Zeke's wing begins to push me gently forward. Trying to resist is not an option. Damn these things are strong. 'I have Susi to thank for showing me the way.'

Uncomfortable with the many eyes now on me, I shuffle nervously. The Alpha Lord's mahogany coloured eyes study me as if he didn't know I was there. Which I know isn't true. He is a predator. He would have assessed me the moment he realised I was here.

'You have given me a gift, human, you have returned my son. I owe you. Anything you require.'

A gift returned.

Gaping, I try to calm my raging thoughts. *He was the gift I had to find.* This whole damn time.

The irony that I nearly ruined it all isn't lost on me.

A small cough beside draws me back to the present.

Steeling my spine, I step out of Zeke's hold.

Mustering up all of my courage, I curtsey and pull the jewel from my neck and watch the mighty males eyes widen.

The whispering in the garden stops.

Alpha Lord Micheal looks sharply at Zeke but I have no time to decipher what it might mean.

'Alpha Lord Michael, I am here to save my father. The King.'

CHAPTER SIXTY SIX

Finishing my story, I take a long swig of the wine I was served when invited to sit with the Alpha Lord and his wife.

Holding the blanket one of the females draped over my shoulders, I sit awkwardly, waiting for a response.

Zeke told me not to hold back. To tell his parents everything. So I did. It's left me feeling a bit raw and vulnerable.

Zeke is standing with what I can assume to be warriors. At least, they sure look like warriors.

Scarier than any I have ever seen at the castle though. Big and bulky with wings that sit large and magnificent on their backs.

There is also long, sharp swords along their spines, just like how Zeke wears his.

There is a heartbeat of silence while my words settle around the table.

I don't blame them, I did just ask if I could get some blood from the Alpha Lord, so I guess silence is expected.

'You were visited by a messenger,' Zeke's mother, Lidiya, says. She is really nice. Offered me food and wine and when it became apparent that Zeke and I were nursing some wounds, she called for a healer. Her fussing was sweet and highlighted that I have some issues. The entire time she was moving us through the pristine gardens and into comfy seats, I was waiting for her to turn on me. To start interrogating what I was doing and why I'm here. I guess I can thank my lovely step-mother for that.

Zeke stayed close the entire time, which helped.

'You are a very special individual it seems. We are lucky to have you here and part of our flock.'

Smiling through my confusion, I have no idea what she means or why Zeke coughs like he just choked on air.

Lidiya grins and throws me a wink. Gods, these beings are a little weird. It's taking all my princess training to sit here politely and look to be understanding the way they speak and interact.

They're so happy and they touch all the time. The Alpha Lord continually brushes his hand on his wife's knee or arm or face. Even the warriors embraced Zeke like they were family. They might be, I guess I don't know. I just know that I've never been in such an affectionate environment before.

The emerald sits heavily around my neck, on full display. When I tried to tuck it back into my ruined, wet shirt, Zeke stopped me.

'You have given me a great deal to think about, Princess Susyri.' The Alpha Lord stands. I mimic the action. Years of training dictates I do.

The Lady Lidya grins like I've done something funny. She hasn't risen but sits comfortable drinking her wine.

'You are welcome here, Princess. Please, rest for now. I can have food sent to your rooms. In the morning, we will discuss your request.' The Alpha Lord indicates behind me and I quickly look over to see two women moving towards us.

'With all due respect, Alpha Lord, I don't have until tomorrow morning. My father is gravely ill. The longer I wait, the higher the chance that I will fail.'

Afraid that I have offended the male who now frowns deeply, I try not to lose my courage.

'You are so eager to return to your kingdom. You don't wish to stay with us for a while. Heal from your injuries?'

Zeke and his father make eye contact. I can't decipher what passes between them.

'You understand that Ezekiel is not allowed to leave these mountains again? You leave here and you leave him. Do you understand that?'

Oh Gods. My stomach plummets into my feet. I hesitate. Leaving Zeke, forever. The idea breaks my heart. It shatters it into a million pieces.

My eyes frantically seek the male who has become so important to me and what I find is not what I expect. I expect him to be annoyed at my hesitation. Angry after what he has done for me. Instead, he nods reassuringly, like he has known this would be how our time together would end. Me choosing my duty, my kingdom and responsibilities, over him.

'I...I can't abandon my quest.' This is torture. I'd rather face the dragon again.

I hate being the centre of attention and every single eye in this garden is on me.

'You have duty and honour, Princess Susyri.' The Alpha Lord bows and I swallow the bile that rises in my throat. I feel like I've betrayed my own heart by uttering those words. 'I grant your request.'

The leader of the Ekalus snaps his fingers and a warrior steps forward and hands him a vial. My head is spinning watching him cut his palm and then fill it with his blood.

Handing it over, I take the offering with a shaking hand.

Gripping the vial, I study the tiny glass bottle in wonder. Everything that I have been through. All the madness and the attacks and the pain—for this.

'Thank you, Alpha Lord.'

'I will have Luke drop you home when you are ready. We will give you a moment to say your farewells. Zeke can let Luke know when you wish to depart. Safe travels, Princess Susyri. You always have a home and friends here with the Ekalus.'

And then they all leave me.

All but one.

CHAPTER SIXTY SEVEN

We just stare.
     Both of us lost. In pain. In grief.

Clearly he's trying to work through the fact that this is goodbye. Just like I am.

That this is the true end of the road.

There is so much that hasn't been said. So much that needs to be fixed between us. Now, there isn't enough time to do any of that.

'It's okay, Susi. You made the right choice. Your loyalty is one of the things I love about you.'

I love about you. He said love. 'Zeke, I...' rushing forward, I throw myself at him, knowing in my soul that he will catch me.

He does effortlessly. Wrapping my arms and legs around him, I hold on tightly, his wing feathers brush against my limbs and I don't feel the need to recoil. In fact, I want to touch.

But first, I crush my lips against his and melt into our kiss. His tongue invades my mouth. His hands grip my butt and I push against him, wanting...no, needing more.

Zeke breaks the kiss and I find myself following his lips like a person starved. His deep growl vibrates against my body.

I love it.

'This could be our last time together for a while.'

I want to remind him that I don't live as long as he does and that with him not being able to leave, and really no way for me to come back, this might be it.

'Yeah,' I say instead and then hold on tight when he tells me to. Bending his knees, Zeke pushes off the ground and before I can shriek in fright, we are airborne.

Head buried in his shoulder, I'm practically digging my nails into his skin. We are flying.

'You're going to miss it.'

'I don't care,' I shout over the rushing wind and hear his musical laughter in the air.

We land with a small thud and I quickly look up to see that we're on what seems to be a balcony. It's attached to a sandstone building. It's gorgeous.

The moon is nearly at its peak and lights up the entire mountain.

Sitting back a little, confident that Zeke will hold me, I take in the scenery. We are on the side of a mountain and I can see buildings and balcony's scattered along the sheer mountain face.

It's a sight I know not many humans get the chance to see.

However, the most breathtaking sight is the male holding me. He is the one that my gaze keeps drifting back to.

Gods his wings...without overthinking anything, I reach over his shoulder. Patting the feathers at the top of his wing, I watch in wonder when he shivers. They aren't soft like I though they'd be. They are rough, reinforcing that they're not there for decoration.

Getting stuck in that ever-green stare once I'm done, I eat my bottom lip. 'Sorry, I should've asked,' I whisper, feeling his gaze like a caress. It's intense and full of emotion.

'Princess, you can touch me anywhere you want. Any time you want. Now come, we can't send you home looking like this and I'm sure you'd love a bath.'

'A bath! Yes! Yes, please!'

Zeke chuckles as I jump off him and instruct him to the way.

CHAPTER SIXTY EIGHT

I'm in Zeke's home. He doesn't have rooms, he has an entire...what did he call it—nest.

That word did some crazy things to my heart.

Half the space he has shown me doesn't have a roof.

I love it.

The only parts of the nest that have ceilings is when we walked to the back where the sleeping quarters are. It takes me way too long to realise that this section has been built into the mountain.

Zeke leads me back to the roof-less section after my tour comes to an end. I know there is more to see, but we don't have the time.

I'm still overwhelmed and miss everything he says as he leads me through a long corridor.

Opening another beautifully crafted door, Zeke flicks a switch and allows me a moment to stare in stunned awe at the way the fire-torches along the wall spring to life. The light reveals a breathtaking bathing room of white. The left wall is all glass panels and even in the darkness reveals the mountains and the Ekalus beasts flying freely.

That hasn't got my attention though. It's the massive bath in the centre of the space. Already full. Steam dancing along the surface. And it's big enough for a male, his wings and...me.

My core tightens. I watch hungrily as Zeke moves around, taking off his wet tunic and throwing it on the floor.

Despite the coolness of the night, my face heats until it is almost unbearable.

This could be our last night together.

'It appears to me that you don't have a roof,' I whisper, my voice heavy with need and point up to the bare night sky.

Giving me a thought-stopping smile, Zeke begins to walk to me slowly. I forget to breathe. I forget my name and what I'm doing here.

'You will find there is one. It's just made of the clearest and strongest material we Ekalus have discovered. Unlike glass, it is near impossible to break. Did you not wonder why the nest is so warm?'

Frowning, I consider his words. 'I thought it was warm because I was watching you walk around without a shirt.'

Zeke throws his head back and laughs that sound. I wish I could bottle it up and take it with me when I leave.

I will miss that sound.

Coming up behind me, Zeke wraps me in his arms. Without any of my usual hesitation, I relax into it. 'You,' he purrs, kissing the side of my neck. I bite back my moan. 'Are incredible. You are handling this all so well.' His lips move as his hands slowly push the collar of my shirt to expose my shoulder. I am panting in need.

'I have lots of questions, don't you worry,' I manage to say.

I feel his smile on my skin. 'I don't doubt it. Ask away?'

Gods, how can I think through the mess that is my head and articulate what's bouncing around in there right now. 'Umm...how do you only half-shift? You can have wings but not be full beast. Is it more comfortable for you to be like that?'

'It depends. In our beast form, we are fully free. With our wings, on two legs, we are comfortable. It is when we fully shift to appear more like humans that it can get a bit tricky. Only those with great power can do that.'

Wow. 'You've been doing it for years.'

'I know,' is his smug reply, making me giggle. Damn fool.

Hands on my hips, he doesn't stop his assault on my neck. When his teeth graze a particular spot behind my ear I shout out in surprise and longing.

I felt that right in my core.

'However, I did need to let the shift happen after three or so days.'

That shocks me. 'You did? I never noticed'

'One of the times was when you were attacked by Captain Jorge. I had only just gone for a fly to find my balance and that happened.'

'Right.' I refuse to think about what happened with Captain Jorge and push the images from my mind. 'Do you know what the emerald symbolises?'

He doesn't answer right away.

Before I can press him, he replies with, 'that one, I'm afraid you're going to have to work out on your own.'

My retort dies when his hands begin to pull my soggy pants down my body. I help as best I can without falling to my knees and begging him to hurry and take me.

'Any other questions?'

Yes. Right. The questions. I regret asking any now. He might hurry this along if I was quiet. 'Are you upset that you're back here?'

'No. It was time.'

He steps back and I fear for a moment that I've upset him. Then he appears at my front. His gaze running over my half naked form with a look of pure devotion.

'I want to be very clear here with you, Susyri. I want to have sex with you, here. Now. I want our last few moment to be one of passion and me worshipping your body,' his voice drops and the sound of it is pure sin. 'Do you want the same?'

Closing my eyes, I fight back the onslaught of tears. Tears of loss and grief. Of realising that I've never been treated with such care and love before. I nod.

'Say the words, Susyri. I want your consent.'

'Yes,' I croak out. I overheat at the feel of his finger tracing lines over the mounds of my breasts.

'You have become the centre of my universe. The reason for me to get up in the morning. A taste of the heavens that I will never get used to. Your consent is a privilege and an honour. Your heart is a gift that I will cherish every day of my life.'

I have trouble existing right now. *How can I leave him? Why am I doing this?*

'Zeke.' His name is a pained whisper. A plea for him to touch me fully and rid me of the unbearable heat building inside me.

'Come.' He smiles, taking my hand. 'Let us take a bath.'

CHAPTER SIXTY NINE

Slipping off my undergarments, I'm very aware of the male watching as I step down into the monstrous pool of a bath.

I take each grey, stone step slowly, and maybe swing my hips a little. My muscles relaxing instantly at the heat of the fragrant liquid.

I dip under and come back up fully relaxed and swim lazily to the far glass panelled wall, fascinated by what is outside.

I've missed baths.

Gasping, I touch the warm glass. 'It's a sliding door,' I announce like the owner of the bathing room doesn't know that the pool-bath extends outside to the balcony I can see illuminated outside.

'No one can see us.'

Squealing at the voice now directly behind me, I spin and come face to face with Zeke. His deep chuckle fills my world. 'Sorry, did I scare you?'

'I didn't realise you were behind me...' I stumble on the last few words as I become hypnotised by the sight before me.

Zeke is naked in the water with me.

Within arm's reach.

Close. So, so close.

Unable to help myself, I follow a droplet of water that runs down his neck and over his defined peck. The physical need to lick it from his sun-kissed skin is almost painful.

'Even if you're bathing in the middle of the day, no one could see in, but if you want to swim outside, I encourage you to wear some kind of clothing.'

'What?' I frown, having lost the ability to hear while my mind conjures up images of licking every surface of his skin. His hardness juts out between us, the clear water not hiding anything. Making me salivate. Making heat pool between my legs.

I'm ready for him.

I don't fight it when he pulls me against his hard body. 'You are so beautiful.'

I think I'm falling more in love with the male with each passing heartbeat. The weight of the issues from the quest and what I have to do soon slip away.

'Kiss me, Zeke,' I plead, needing him right now more than I need air to breathe.

His wings expand in the water. The bath big enough to accommodate the breathtaking span of them.

Blocking the entire room from sight, Zeke walks us until my back is trapped between the warm glass panel and his hard, hot body. His hands take the impact and I gasp at the power being emitted into the room.

'Your wish is my command, Princess.' And on that, he kisses me.

It's sweet and unhurried to begin and then grows in intensity.

My arms fly over his shoulders and when he grips my butt to lift me, I wrap my legs around his middle. The water is still unnaturally hot against our skin as we grind into each other. Our kiss now all teeth and tongue.

When he pulls back to position himself at my entrance, he waits. 'Are you sure you want this?'

'Yes,' I demand, not fully in control of my emotions. I've waited for this for such a long time.

His growl fills the room and I throw my head back, hitting the glass and cry out at the sheer pleasure of him filling me.

In and in, he pushes.

Claiming me.

Branding me from the inside out.

Ruining me.

Staking a claim that I know will never be filled again.

Eyes locked in those ever-green depths, I'm powerless to control the single tear that drips down my face when he declares, 'I love you, Susyri. I couldn't say it before knowing I was keeping this from you. I love you with each breath that I take. I have loved you from the moment I laid eyes on you and will love you until I leave this world. You are mine, Susyri. Forever.'

I see the words he has just uttered on his face. The depths of his emotions matching my own.

He is mine and even if this is the last time I see him, I'll always be his. No one can compare.

'I love you, Zeke. I will love you until my dying breath and into the afterlife. I am yours, forever, and you will always live in my heart.'

His scent caresses my skin, his wings shutter and relax into the water and I come with the first thrust of his hips.

His answering moan igniting the fire in my body. My soul.

He takes me hard and fast. Pushing me up and over the peak of pleasure, over and over again.

CHAPTER SEVENTY

It is heavy night by the time Zeke and I finally let Luke know that I'm ready to return to my kingdom.

Heartbroken and in tears, I asked Zeke to stay inside his nest while I walked to where Luke is waiting on the balcony.

The tall Ekalus Warrior bows at the hips when I approach, concern filtering over his face when he asks if I am sure I want to go.

The handful of steps it takes me to get to him are the hardest I've ever walked.

'Yes,' I croak, tapping the vial of blood I secured in the top pocket of the butter-soft leather jacket Zeke insisted that I take.

It's too big on me but it smells like sunshine and it will be a treasure I worship for the rest of my life.

Zeke and I said our goodbyes when we finally found our way out of the pool-bath.

It was hard and full of ugly tears and I made him swear that he'd not come out while I left, or I was afraid I'd change my mind.

Hand brushing the emerald securely placed under the tunic a beautiful Ekalus female bought over for me to wear, I almost lose my focus and run back inside. I tried to leave it, having assumed it was important to the Alpha Lord and was told to keep it. That it was mine.

Luke waits patiently.

I just…I can't. Not yet.

'Zeke,' I call out, spinning around and realising that he is on the other side of the glass, watching me. 'I love you.' They are simple words and I hope he can see how much this pains me and how sorry I am for choosing duty over him. Over happiness.

Turning is difficult. Luke bends and lifts me into his arms with permission and I hate them on my body. They aren't Zeke's arms. It feels wrong being in another's embrace.

'Are you ready?' he asks and I know there is more he wants to say.

No. No. No. 'Yes.' It's like ripping my own heart out and leaving it behind when he takes off.

We arrive just as the sun is beginning to rise.

The flight was silent and awkward and Luke was nothing but a gentleman the entire trip. Landing on the roof of my father's castle, the male seems to blend into the darkness still clinging to the walls. It makes me question a great deal seeing how comfortable he is flying into human territory.

There are guards everywhere. Oblivious, silly humans.

'I leave you, Lady.' Luke bows one last time before he takes off, not waiting for a reply.

Wiping at my tears, I hurry into the castle, at speed, not fully registering that I am back, or that everything feels so different. Not physically. The walls are still made of stone and the guards are where they are supposed to be, but the feel of this place. Me in this place.

I'm different.

Running past the gaping outright stares of the nobles and soldiers that I pass, I pray that I'm not too late.

I come to a screeching halt before my father's rooms and push open the heavy doors. They crash open and everybody in the space jumps to their feet.

Eyes scanning the stunned crowd, I find what I'm looking for and thank the heavens when I see that my father is still breathing.

'You!' a shrill cry bounces off the stone walls making me flinch.

Ignoring the Queen, I hurry towards the bed and come face-to-face with a wall of soldiers.

Glaring up at them, I almost laugh at how pathetically weak they all appear. I have just been in the arms of an Ekalus Warrior. I have faced Wolven and Xaver and a damn dragon to be here.

'Move out of my way.'

The Queen and her soldier's back off with whatever they see on my face, their eyes like fire as they scan my embellished pants, the oversized leather jacket covering my torso.

I can't seem to care. They can think what they want.

It's refreshing and invigorating.

Pushing my way past the mass of mourners watching over the dying King, I sit on the bed beside my father.

Nobody moves to stop me. Nobles spill into the rooms to see what is happening. My name is whispered in hushed tones. I've been gone for so long. They thought I was dead.

Pulling the vial out of my pocket, I uncork the gift given to me by the Alpha Lord. Some healer starts demanding to know what I'm doing. Demanding that I tell them what I have. I even think they try to stop me on the Queen's demand, but I'm not listening and Master Kieran is now standing guard over me, threatening to kill anyone who lays a hand on me. I didn't even notice he was in the room.

My father rouses slightly, his eyes cracking open just a sliver so that he can understand what is going on and I truly hope he does because I need him to cooperate. This room smells like decay and death.

'Drink this father,' I instruct and lift his head. Helping him, I monitor every drop as it spills into his mouth and down his throat. When the vial is empty, my father closes his eyes again and passes-out.

I finally sit back.

It's over.

My quest is complete.

I did it.

I travelled along the Tilman Road and into the Dead Forest. I found the gift returned, got past the monster guarding the road to Ekalus Peak. I faced the Alpha Lord and told him my story. He gifted me his blood and I've returned and saved my father's life. Along the way, I fell in love.

True, endless love. I made friends. I experienced pain and fear like no other. I found strength I didn't know I had. I fought and I won. I laughed and I cried. And I danced in the rain.

I did everything the Messenger told me to do, and more.
Now what?

CHAPTER SEVENTY ONE

It's been three months and so much has changed.

Yet, everything is still the same.

Picking at the food on my plate, I listen to the next noble who has come up to the King's table to congratulate him on the advantageous betrothal between his daughter and the Highben Lord. It's not directed to me, the one actually getting married—supposedly.

It's getting harder and harder to pretend.

I have a bag packed in my rooms for later tonight. The marriage ceremony is in a few days and I'll not be here for it. I refuse. I've already made my opinion known and despite the fact that I saved my father's life, neither he, nor the Queen, care about my requests.

I really dislike all of them. However, my quest is complete. My father is alive and there is no more talk of who will rule.

The castle is calmer.

Talks of successors and threats are gone from the halls and the Queen has been put back in her place.

The problem is, going back to normality means that my life is exactly how it was before…everything happened. Before the quest. Before…Zeke.

I'm expected to act the way I did and accept the things that I once accepted. I'm being forced to forget my quest and live this stifling life.

The restraints of the castle have been suffocating. I don't find pleasure in going down to the training fields. I've been given new rooms in the castle and have new advisors that have been managing my life and my betrothal for the last three months. Every action I make is scrutinised by them, every event I refuse to attend complained about, and every time I tell them that I couldn't care less about my upcoming wedding to Hamish Highben, I'm scowled at.

Grief has been eating at me. Day by day, I feel myself slipping into misery. I miss Zeke with every piece of my soul. I curl up in my bed every night, hugging his jacket and the emerald wishing to have a way to contact him.

I fired my maid, Anna, the moment I got back and told her to never grace my doorstep again and have only eaten my meals with Father Fredrick and Master Kieran. It has been good to be around them again, though I see now that they treat me like I'm a little girl. Everyone has been weird about my recent decisions to change my maid and apparently even the way I speak now offends the people around me. I guess I do cuss a little more and I don't hold back when I'm annoyed. The Tilman Road has rubbed off on me, and I like it.

I'm not the bastard princess.

Not anymore.

Which is what they'll discover when my chambers are empty in the morning. I hope to maybe find Henry and the others. Head back on the Tilman Road. Potentially find Toppin.

For now, I will sit and eat and fake-smile at nobles who think they possess power, while my 'future husband' is beside my father at the main table. His full head of hair is styled like a wave atop his head and his brows thin and curved. He is attractive, if you like that kind of thing. Tall-ish, brown eyes. Soft skin. Lean.

Unfortunately, I don't.

I want my man to laugh at me when I say something stupid. To tease me and joke about things that shouldn't be funny. I want a man with wings who says things like 'you're the centre of my universe'.

I'm sitting right at the back of the hall, on a table assigned to me by the Queen, who clearly forgot that this is my betrothal ceremony.

Contemplating faking a headache and going back to my rooms, my attention catches on the minstrels that stand before my father. It doesn't take long to realise that I know the storyteller from the road. The one in all the taverns.

No longer wanting to escape so quickly, I sit listening, until my ears begin to ring and my stomach churns at the story that comes from his lips.

It's the one I heard before.

One that has new meaning as I grip the emerald I have safely tucked into the fabric binding my breasts.

AL ROJO

'Some say the young village woman was walking in the meadow,
Some say she was at the river where the current flows,
But this bard knows it was nothing as grand.
Working in her garden, she simply dug up the jewel, it's colour of blood
and dirty sand.
'Perplexed, she sat, and examined the piece, that burnt hot in her palm,
yet soothed.
For days, she waited at her table alone, she felt the tide of impending
doom.
It called to something, she knew in her bones, and her heart pounded
just out of beat. Until one day he came, with wings of red, and declared
her the source of his heat.
'Shocked the young woman rejected the claim and yet the beast of
firewings didn't move.
He waited and watched and tended her fields, his devotion he wanted to
prove.
No word or demand would deter him, oh no.
You see, unbeknownst to her, the girl found a heartstone.
A rare treasure that won her his heart.'

CHAPTER SEVENTY TWO

The grip I have over the emerald is biting. My heart pounds to the beat of the music.

The hall erupts, begging for more.

It's just a muffle of noise.

Words spoken between Zeke and I flood my mind. Conversations that never made much sense at the time.

The bard, pleased with his audience, bows once more and I finally notice the woman standing beside him, playing the small string instrument.

Her long white-blonde hair flows around a dress of green.

The music starts up again and I suck in a breath when her silver eyes meet mine and she smiles knowingly.

I gasp loudly.

Up next is a poem I remember.

AL ROJO

'I'll tell you a tale, a tale of old,

Where the wings didn't scare you,

And the women were bold.

Where a beast of the sky,

Was every lover's dream,

And being alone was the reason to die.

You see,

An Ekalus is a one-woman show,

A love for the ages,

A stone he'd bestow.

A treasure that marks,

A soul with a soul,

A stone to bind two hearts,

It is their ultimate goal.

For only a pair,

can make two a three,

And that is where fate is not fair,

A rare gift is an Ekalus babe-ee.

But beware,

Sweet audience,

For the stories are true,

Death will be waiting,

If you touch a heartstone,

That is not meant for you.'

The emerald is in my hand before I can process what I'm doing and I study the jewel with a newfound awareness. 'Death will be waiting if you touch a heartstone that is not meant for you,' I whisper, reliving that moment with Captain Jorge.

A heartstone. That can't be possible.

Zeke touched it all the time...he...Oh my Gods.

I might be mistaken but the messenger playing the instrument nods at me like she knows I have just worked it out.

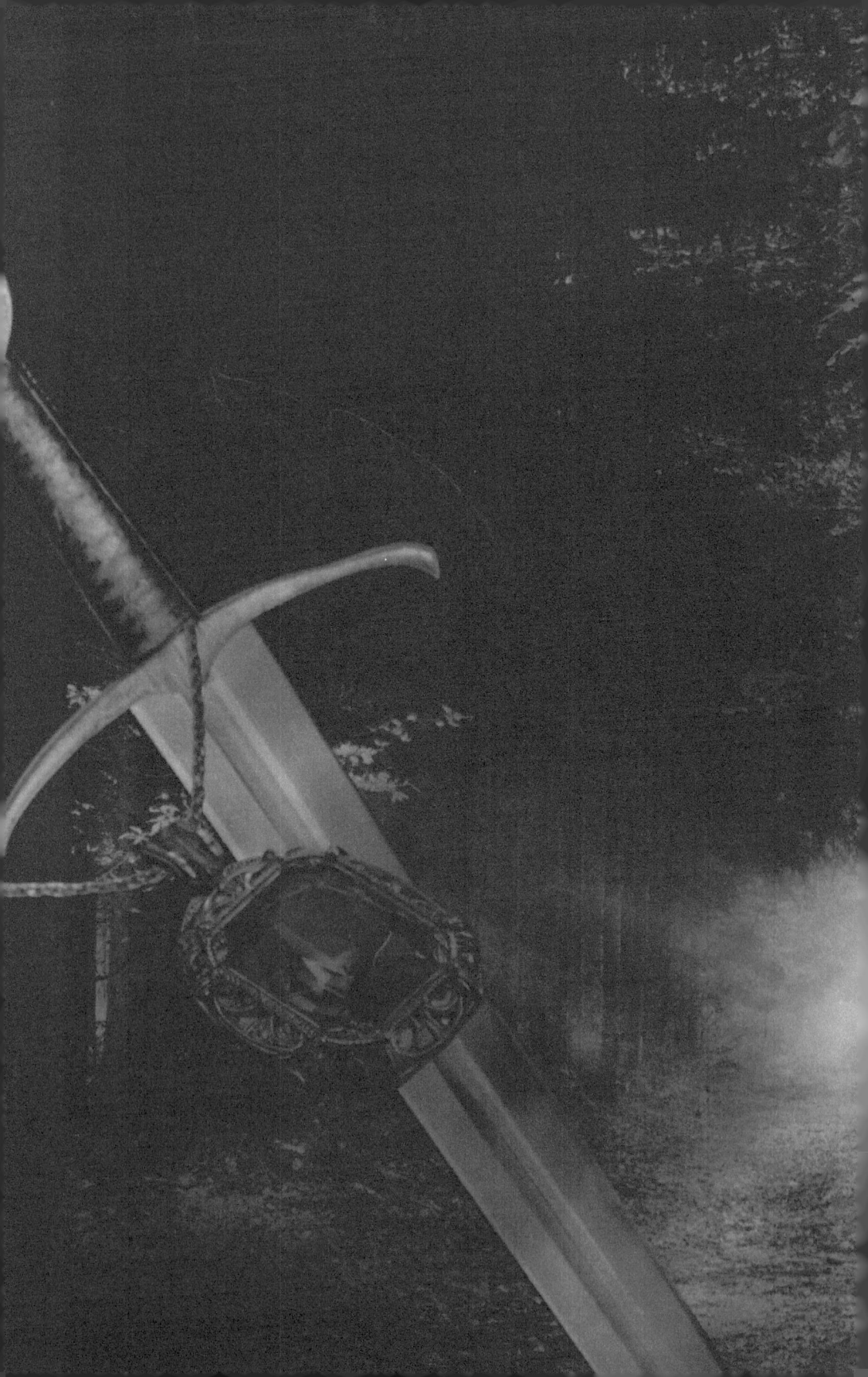

CHAPTER SEVENTY THREE

My heart is a mess. I don't even acknowledge the shadow that looms over my table or that the Queen begins to spurt her hatred in my direction. Passively-aggressive, of course.

She's spurting some shit about how she doesn't believe that I found the elixir that saved the King. She thinks I have allies or something. It's obviously eating her up.

Using all my strength to push down the need to rage out and rip her hair out, I manage to get a hold of myself.

Smiling my best smile, I realise that I no longer hate the woman who begins to insult me in front of the nobles standing around her. Their laughter so forced that I actually feel sorry for her; because I see it now. I see what the shame my birth must have caused, my presence a constant reminder of what her husband did. And what she couldn't do.

What a sad, miserable life she leads.

She is nothing to me.

I just found out something so life altering that I feel sorry that all she has in life is my father. Someone who I gave up everything for. And all I got was a few rooms in the castle like that was a massive gift to thank me.

It doesn't matter though. It truly doesn't.

'Are you even listening, you daft girl!'

'No,' I reply sweetly, telling the truth. 'I wasn't.'

She scowls and it does nothing for her. 'I said I can't wait to ship you off with the Highben's where you can be their problem. It's going to be—'

The force of the being that slams into the ground behind the Queen shakes the entire hall.

It takes a heartbeat before everyone registers what has just joined our gathering. The screaming starts and then stops abruptly when wings of deep brown, lined with mahogany, pull back to reveal a man so perfect, he glows.

The creature stands to his full height. His magnificent wings spread wide before they snap against his back.

People scramble away from the centre of the room. There are bodies squashed in piles around the perimeter of the space.

The Ekalus' face is a mask of pure rage as he looks around.

His eyes fall on my table, on the Queen now immobile, standing over me, and then to the King who has risen from his decorative chair on the other side of the room.

No one speaks. Or if they do, I don't hear it.

He is here.

'You are right, Susi,' Zeke says, ever-green eyes locked on mine. His voice booms through the space. Commanding and full of power. I've missed that sound. Dreamt about it constantly. 'Her voice *is* really annoying. Want me to get rid of her for you?' he asks, only I can see the twinkle of humour under the predatory mask he wears.

There is no mistaking who he is referring to and every wide eyed human now gapes unbelievingly in my direction.

'Not right now, thank you, Ezekiel.' I smile. There are dramatic gasps that have me laugh. My emotions are rolling. I begin to shake under the pressure of them.

How is he here? He can't be. The Alpha Lord said he had to stay in Ekalus Peak.

I catch my wobbling lip and grip the emerald harder. It cuts into my skin.

'Come,' he demands, holding out a hand to me, clearly loving the attention and the fear in the room. 'There is a feast happening in the halls of the Ekalus and I'm bored. I need my human companion to provide me some entertainment.'

The way he says entertainment has my stomach clench and my thighs press together. 'Entertainment huh?'

He winks and heat settles in my core. Every step I make is tracked. Someone is yelling. Maybe my father. Maybe the entire hall. None of it matters.

I take Zeke's outstretched hand and go willingly into his embrace. He pulls me flush against him and every nerve in my body erupts. It's like coming home. Like finding where I truly belong.

'How are you here?' I'm still in shock and lean into the hand he runs over my face as if trying to remember what I feel like. Like he has missed my touch as much I have missed his.

'My father got sick of my moping around and told me to come and get you so that I can be useful to our people again.' Laughing, I feel all the pain and tension leave my body. 'If you will have me, Princess?'

Opening my hand, I show him what is in it but Zeke doesn't look. He seems to already know. 'I worked out the meaning of the emerald.'

'You did?' he asks, studying my face expectantly. There is humour and hunger in his gaze. It is hard to remember what I'm saying.

'Yes. It's a heartstone.' I watch his reaction with so much focus that the rest of the hall blurs around the edges. I'm aware of people running away and I think there are soldiers pulling out weapons, but none make a step towards Zeke.

The Ekalus Warrior doesn't seem to care.

'It's your heartstone, Ezekiel.'

I wait for him to deny it.

He doesn't.

The smile that fills his face brightens my life. 'Yes, Susyri. It is my heartstone. A stone given to me the day I came of age. A stone that is part of my soul to be held by my one true mate.' A tear slips down my cheek. Mate. While the word isn't used by us humans, it seems right. Fitting. It is what I feel. I'm his mate and he is mine. 'You have owned my heart from the moment you held this jewel in your hand and will own every part of me forever.'

Oh Gods.

'I have missed you,' I exclaim. My face is beginning to hurt, I'm smiling so wide.

Zeke's face gets all serious. His hand runs through my hair before wiping the water from my face. 'Oh, Susi, you have no idea how much I've missed you. Every day has been like living without a piece of my soul.'

'Take me home, Zeke,' I plead.

'You will call Ekalus Peak home, my mate?' Zeke's gaze is so intense.

'I will call wherever you are home, Ezekiel.' And I mean it, from the bottom of my heart.

Zeke nods, his focus on me and only me. He makes me feel like I am the only one in the world. 'What say you to going on our own quest? A quest through life, together.'

More tears come. 'I'd like that.'

Zeke grins and grabs the emerald. He slips the chain over my head and picks me up. I squeal and then bury my nose into his neck and breathe in the scent of him. I missed it so much. His leather jacket lost the smell weeks ago.

Zeke seems to finally realise that there are people watching us. He stretches out his wings and takes notice of the room. 'What is this celebration for?'

'My betrothal.'

Zeke finds that hilarious. His booming laughter fills the space. 'You've been my mate from the moment you wore this stone, Princess. This means nothing to me.' His eyes fix on something across the room.

My father. The King watches us with a devout of emotion.

'Let's go, Zeke. We have a quest to start.'

'Yes, Toppin is missing you and I believe we have been invited to a wedding between Fi and Calligan in a few weeks.'

My heart swells. The future, for once, looks bright.

With a mighty beat of his wings, Zeke flies us into the sky and into a world full of new possibilities and new adventures. A new life where I am no longer a bastard princess, but a mate to an Ekalus warrior with ever-green eyes.

Ezekiel.

My Zeke.

About the AUTHOR

A L Rojo is an author, educator, wife and mother who lives in Sydney, Australia. From a young age, she understood the power of getting lost in a good book. After giving herself permission to explore her creativity, she found that she loved writing novels that focus on strong female characters, love, spice, and the wonderful complexities of life. Her goal is to simply create worlds where anyone can escape into, for however long they may need. She says that along this journey she has left behind a piece of herself in every character she creates.

To get the latest updates, follow A L Rojo on:

Website: www.alrojo.com.au

Facebook: A L Rojo

Instagram: alrojo_writer

www.ingramcontent.com/pod-product-compliance
Lightning Source LLC
LaVergne TN
LVHW090150080526
838201LV00116BA/854